NAME THE BABY

MARK CIRINO

NAME THE BABY

ANCHOR BOOKS

DOUBLEDAY

NEW YORK

LONDON

TORONTO

SYDNEY

AUCKLAND

AN ANCHOR BOOK
PUBLISHED BY DOUBLEDAY
a division of Bantam Doubleday Dell Publishing Group, Inc.
1540 Broadway, New York, New York 10036

ANCHOR BOOKS, DOUBLEDAY, and the portrayal of an anchor are trademarks of
Doubleday, a division of Bantam Doubleday Dell Publishing Group, Inc.

Name the Baby was first published in Great Britain in 1997 by Phoenix House/Wei-
denfeld and Nicolson/The Orion Publishing Group. The Anchor Books edition is
published by arrangement with Phoenix House.

Book design by Fritz Metsch

The quotations from "Prodigal Son" and "Growin' Up" by Bruce Springsteen are
used by special permission of Jon Landau Management. All rights reserved. The
quotation by Pete Townshend is reprinted by permission. Copyright © *Rolling Stone,*
5 November 1987. The excerpt from Kazuo Ishiguro's *The Remains of the Day* is
reprinted by permission of the author, c/o Rogers, Coleridge & White Ltd., 20 Powis
Mews, London W11 1JN; originally published in hardcover in Great Britain by Faber
and Faber Ltd., London, and in the United States by Alfred A. Knopf, Inc., New
York, in 1989. Copyright © 1988 by Kazuo Ishiguro.

Library of Congress Cataloging-in-Publication Data

Cirino, Mark, 1971–
    Name the baby / Mark Cirino. — 1st Anchor Books ed.
      p.   cm.
    I. Title.
    PS3553.I75N3   1998
    813'.54—dc21   97-41134
                                            CIP

ISBN 0-385-49159-X

Printed in the United States of America

First Anchor Books Edition: June 1998

10 9 8 7 6 5 4 3 2 1

to David Fox

I wish I knew, really knew, your language of months

THE MULLIGANS, "Nina, Nina"

NIGHT BUS HOME

I've got a good imagination, man, that's the problem. The way it is now, I can't turn anywhere in this place, without hearing echoes of the falsetto gasp, without seeing some crazy flash of silver, without somehow actually sensing the anger of that miniature explosion. Know what? Cop was right there, thinkin' he was doin' me a favor explaining the whole thing to me, and the bastard told me, cool as a veteran newscaster, that, scientifically speaking, her eyes imploded. Now let me get this straight, he had to go ahead and tell me that? Can you believe that shit? Her sad eyes. I guess they had to give in; things can only stand so much.

After all, I was the one who got to see her dead before anyone, and I could swear I saw the look of surprise on her face—shock—like she didn't expect the fuckin' gun to go off in the first place, or the bullet to hit her or hurt her. She didn't expect it? Well then what was she thinking when she crammed the thing in her mouth? What exactly was she thinking? Tell me this, who has the nerve to commit suicide, and then try to play it off like an ambush? Would you? But I mean, these falsetto screams everywhere, and I know, just know what it sounded like, those kinds of thoughts just make this place kind of useless for me at this point. I got no purpose stickin' around here, pretending nothing ever happened. Word travels fast, and I don't need neighbors glaring at me like it's my fault or something, like I gave her the gun, or showed her how to use it, or suggested the whole stupid idea in the first place, or something like that. People talk and talk. I look right back at 'em sometimes, but what for? What's the point? It's so hard to change people's minds about certain things, and the ones whose minds you can change, well they probably aren't worth having on your side anyway. Someone from school said I should go to this survivor's group that meets somewhere in the city, just to check it out, but I didn't want to hear anything about it. You don't know me, but trust me, that's not really what I'm about, groups and shit. I certainly don't feel like a survivor anyway, kid, I got no faith in any plan that comes in a booklet or pamphlet, or something. All I think I can do is let it flow, let it breathe; used to be our place, now it's just me. See, that's the thing, I know it's just me, but certain things still occur to me all of a sudden, right out of nowhere—like how I know I was the last thing on her mind, 'cause I saw it on her permanent expression, the only one she can't hide—and I can see right before she did it, I know the way she shook her head, like when she's totally fed up and through talking for the night, real subtle, the way she always did it. And I can see that big inhale, right before she's going to scream or make some huge statement, which, face facts, she definitely did.

But this place? Here? I mean, how'm I supposed to stick around? When I came back that night, *Hendrix Essential*— disc two—was looped on the CD-player, must have been playing for fuckin' hours, blasting, driving the neighbors insane. That's probably the real reason why the neighbors hate me, come to think of it—the suicide inconvenienced them. But do you know anyone that kills themselves to Jimi Hendrix? I mean, is that what you're supposed to do? How'm I supposed to put Hendrix on now? I can't listen to Hendrix again, I can't make love again, can't argue politics or life again—all that stuff is just ruined forever. Ah, what am I talking about? Sure I can—I can do whatever it is I got to do—just not in this motherfucker of an apartment. No way. No I can't. Not right now. And so? And so I'm out the door.

Check me out, man, boundin' down the steps, flyin' down the block. I'm gonna figure everything out. Gonna finally figure out why when someone else dies, your own life ends up passin' before you—that's always kind of freaked me out. A night like this, you got no destination; anywhere beats where you were, that's for sure. Hey, maybe after all this it might not even be so bad to get my ass back to the old house, back to New Jersey, come to think of it. I got a call the other night from the folks, and they said they knew how I felt, and that they were there for me, and all the kind of strange things that folks say. But I guess they really were, in fairness, and I guess that parents are a refuge in a weird kind of way, so might as well use them. And maybe I will, eventually. On the answering machine, Mom had the thin, hollow voice she must have manufactured special for the occasion. I know Dad was rehearsing the most Dad-like statements custom-made for the situation, too, so I wasn't fazed by his words, no matter what. I mean, let's face it, I really shouldn't harsh on 'em too much—who's to say what you're supposed to tell people anyway, man, I sure didn't write the script.

But check me out, I said, Timberlands on and blurred, 'cause I'm jetting down the block and feeling ready for anything. I'm heading downtown, I know downtown the best. See this workshirt? Wine-red, kid, that's what the lady at the counter said. It's a little roughed up, but it's comfortable as anything. People think you're a slob if you wear these too often, but fuck 'em, I wear this one just about every day, and I might even pick myself up a new one also someday. Gray, I'm thinking. This wine-red one's looking good, though. I know girls don't really like it like this, not tucked in at all (girls like to see *ass*). It's drooping over, half 'cause it's real comfortable like that, and half kind of to cover Leonia's gun. I figure I'd rather keep the thing on me from now on—you never know who'll use it otherwise. Always got that American Indian necklace drooping down, the medallion snuggled between my chest muscles. People wonder why I bother wearin' it if no one can see it, if they can only see the top of the rope (I wear it *under* my shirt, man, always) but I tell 'em don't worry about it—I like the cold metal pressing against my skin. Trust me, it's the way to go. It's proof the shit ain't cosmetic; it's real. And black jeans—what else? Someone told me that blue jeans were invented for the gold rush in 1849 but black jeans weren't invented until much later, just for show, just for looks. I don't buy that for a second, man, black jeans are all I need. Blue jeans start lookin' dirty after a few weeks. I mean, black jeans'll look the same, unless you spill, like, white paint or acid on them or something. And who does that? Plus, I've got a nice short haircut, dude, not like all the other guys my age that pay out the ass, and end up wearing one of those horrible, lame-ass baseball hats anyway, like a sports team or something. But I got no use for that sort of shit. I mean, Leonia used to dig all kinds of sports, but what use do I got for that? You win some, you lose some—it's all mathematics to me, anyway.

One of my worst habits I got a few years back, when I spent the summer in Rome with my psycho cousin, but it's gotten worse in the past week or so. See, let me explain, I love playing harmonica, it's like my favorite thing—I ain't saying I'm the best at it or anything, but I can hang with anyone, you know? I can say what needs to be said. And fuck lessons! Who wants to listen to some old guy explaining how to draw notes or how to lay out when someone solos or how to fuckin' wail when the fifth note kicks in? You think I'm stupid or something, kid? Jesus, you probably think I can't figure shit like that out for myself. Dude, let me give you some advice—put on a Howlin' Wolf or a Jimmy Reed or someone like that, and learn; don't just sit there in some class. Just figure it out for yourself, and make sure you always remember it, like those multiplication tables in fifth grade. Every time someone hears me play they all say the same thing: pretty good! You ever take lessons, man? And I always tell 'em no, because the question they're asking me is, "have you ever sat in a class with a notepad and learned the penta-fuckin'-tonic scale from some expert," which just isn't the case. I mean, that's not how it happened. Yeah, I've read a few books on my own and listened to records, but that's about it. And all the stories in the blues books say these guys all had the same vice—Mr Jack Daniels. And Jack's the bad habit I was talking about in the first place, by the way, not the harmonica.

Well, about Jack, I'm thinking, these old blues guys must know something I don't know, right? I'm not above admitting that. So I step up with my cousin and buy my first fifth of the shit at some Roman liquor store. Oh, it might have hurt like a motherfucker going down, but it got me in the mood to play like you wouldn't believe. I guess you could say it took away my tendency to be embarrassed. There's an American guy I used to know over in Italy who's a poet, a guitar player—cooler than most. So we started pouring glasses one time, making toasts and playing his songs on a starry night on the Piazza di Spagna for all these Italian high school girls. It was the best night I think I've ever had, so Jack and I have been partners ever since. I don't know what happened to that singer dude, come to think of it. He was talking about coming back to America to go to law school, but had enrolled in a course on magic the afternoon I left to come back home. Man, we used to get together for coffee or blues all the time. Really, though, what's the difference between coffee and blues? Well, one's liquid, and the other gets your heart pumpin'. Strange guy; probably law school sucked him in. I should look him up.

But with Jack Daniels, it's not that I have it every day— 'cause I don't—but when I do, man, I go right after it. I don't play games. I'll drink until I'm all fucked up, down, diagonal and dangling. Shit, man, gotta tell you, a couple days ago, after all this Leonia shit went down, I drank over at Down the Hatch, a place to meet college kids, if that's what you're into. I kept drinking whiskeys straight, and kept doin' 'em, and then this one guy I think I met once before started buying them for me, just to see how many I could drink, and I was crackin' people up, so they bought more for me. So after all that, I danced with a few people, mostly girls, and went home. Worst thing I ever did was not throw up, 'cause the next day I could taste the puke way down deep, and my heart was somehow beating all through my head, stretching the skin of my scalp. To tell you the truth, I felt like getting Leonia's gun and ending it myself right then and there. Then I went into the bathroom, got on the toilet, and took a shit that stung like crazy, like it had fangs, and when I wiped there was a dark red chunky mound of blood in the paper. *Flush* that shit, motherfucker!

So when I leave the apartment, you see, I don't need too much—I don't need all these crazy trappings, or anything like that. All I need is a credit card, a cash card, my driver's license, and the harmonica—just my cheap one. Who needs an expensive harmonica? The only thing that ends up making the noise anyway is the air, if you think about it. I stop on my way to wherever over at Jake's Spirits. I love that place because the "s" at the end of that sign was wasted, somehow, I mean, I think someone must have fucked it up somehow. But whoever did it knew what they were doing, because now it says "Jake's Spirit," which is a crack up, because the guy, Jake, behind the damn counter, never moves, never cards, never asks questions, never smiles. Only thing that bastard ever does is have some financial journal open to the stock pages, and read each line of it, one by one, as if he's seriously thinking about investing in every single one of the companies, or something. Makes sense to consider all your options if you're gonna be blowin' all that money, I guess. Now, I don't know too much about them, but investments seem real shady to me. When it comes to gambling my money, I guess you'd have to say I'm pretty conservative—I don't even buy ten-packs of subway tokens, speaking of long-term investments. This is New York City, kid, you never know. But stocks and shit; that stuff is all mathematics, too. Just ain't my kind of mathematics, not like music.

So I pause a little bit to watch the guy watching the paper, and Jake knows I'm here, and knows I know he knows, but the bastard still won't look up unless I get right in his face and I'm looking at every little crater on his cheeks, right up to the counter with my twenty, or whatever, which I finally break down and do. So Jake smirks invisibly and then he plugs in the numbers, holds up a paper bag, stuffs the bottle in there, and then plunges it into my hands. Our eyes meet at last, and he's all silently condescending, like an uncle handing you a ten-spot for leverage later, like he's doin' me some favor not carding me. I'm legal, nobody can touch me. Fact is, I'm twenty-one, I can do just about anything in this country except be president, and you know, I don't think any of us would be all that thrilled if I were, would we?

Something about a bum, man, always gets to me. I'm not trying to be Mario Cuomo or Mother Teresa, but I can't manage to live normally knowing that there are people out there sleeping in a bed of their own cold piss. The interesting thing about urine is that it starts out nice and hot, but turns cold real fast, just like any other liquid. So I see these people here in New York with their sleeping bags of cardboard, wrapped up in any clothes they can scrounge, and I can't just move on. Some people are immune, you know? I guess you can get like that, and just walk on. I gotta talk to 'em, or if I move on, I carry 'em with me for the rest of the day, and that's bad news, 'cause then I tend to scowl and snap a lot, but it's good in the sense that I don't tend to whine too much, unless you count this whole deal about Leonia.

So this bum-type on Fifth Avenue, midtown, somehow catches me on the move on my way downtown, and you know I'm walking fast; it's night, gettin' kind of late, and he *still* sees through my paper bag, and croaks, "Whiskey, young man?" only with no inflections or punctuation or anything like that, so it just comes out in one desperate breath. Hey, what do you think, my whiskey's too good for his ass? Hell, no! So I pour some into his fucked up paper cup—coffee stains and dirt all over the damn thing—and we tap glasses, and I say "ding" out of habit, 'cause the chicks love it when I do that, college chicks at least, and we swallow. That whiskey claws and scratches down my throat and leaves a thin red vertical streak down the center of my throat and chest and stomach, and it's sizzling and angry. Yow, that's about my third or fourth shot, and I'm flying down the block. I touch my ass to make sure my harmonica's still in my rear pocket, which it certainly is. It didn't go anywhere. "Thanks, young man, nice surprise," the bum says again in another blurt, and I smack my lips loudly, a gesture of kindness, then I'm down the block, just like I said.

Ever hear of Terra Blues, the place on Bleecker? I don't know, I guess it's cool enough. Thing is, all the fuckin' sausages'll be there tonight—this ain't the time to go. Who wants to go on a Thursday night when all the fraternity sausages'll be there? I like to go when I'm about the only one in the joint, maybe a lady or two, and Moe Holmes, or Slapmeat, or someone like that is in the house, and they're more rehearsing than performing. Thing about blues, like poetry, in some ways, is that every song is nothing more than an homage to an earlier song or artist. Where's it all start? That ain't for me to say; I got no idea.

I walk by the NYU library, and through the upper-floor windows I can see all the students in there looking over their books, in case the teacher asks them a stumper or something the next day. I didn't even know that thing was open this late. Kind of depressing, because the kids in the windows were probably compelled to work instead of go out, yet they chose a seat next to the window, as kind of a compromise with themselves. Like, every few pages they can look out and see people like me with *plans*. I don't like to see those kids in there, 'cause I think it's a nice enough night, and I mean, the blues are in the air, at least they are for me, man. Now, I like to read, don't get me wrong, it's just that there's a time and place for all things under the sun—even philosophy. Oh, you like philosophy, too? Hegel, right? I knew it! I pinned you for Hegel a mile away, kid. So I take one last shot—right there in public, right there in front of whatever security guards there are over at NYU—I think they're just grad students or something, to be honest, looking for a couple credits. So, again with one more last shot and the bottle is damn near drained—did it all myself except for the drink I poured the bum and the little bit that spilled to the right side of my mouth which I wiped off with my wine-red work-shirt, and I purposely graze my back pocket once more, just to make sure my harp is still there, which it is. Damn, how much is the cover for Terra, come to think of it, like three?

So I'm up the stairs to Terra and flying, feeling really loose, really good. As usual, the whiskey is working. I can hear the clinks of the glasses before I can hear the chords or drums, so things might not be smoking yet. The bouncer looks at me funny, but I look past him, like I'm meeting someone in there. What he knows, I might be another sausage. I don't even look that different from those guys, except my clothes and the expression on my face; that is, I actually have one. Leonia loved blues music, and I laid beside her one night on the top of Col di Piuma overlooking Il Duomo in Florence, watching that golden building glow to the highest heavens, shining right into the whites of her eyes, and glinting off the silver of my harmonica, which I had with me. I was whispering the lyrics to "Before You Accuse Me" and letting my swaying harmonica moan in between the lines. It's kind of a mean song, but Leonia knew better back then—she didn't take any of those lines personally, I don't think. I mean, I didn't write the tune, anybody knows that. Kills me to think of that night. She called me "romantic" for the first and only time that night.

What? Romantic? All we did was make love outside, near a cemetery, under the stars of Tuscany and beside an empty cardboard box of wine (2,000 lire, kid—like less than two bucks). That's what women call romantic? Can't figure them out. I read this literature criticism book for a class that said romantic meant "of the senses," and I do believe that's true, because I was feeling it that night as much as ever, and you know what? Strangely, I'm feeling it again tonight. Different circumstances, but, yeah, romantic, that's what I'm feeling, up for exercisin' my senses. So I bump the burly guy four at the door, minimal eye contact, and I'm through. Good thing I got rid of the empty Jack, or they wouldn't have me here. Only well-behaved blues fans, I guess. Sorry, left my letter sweater at home, but I'm a forgetter, for worse or for better.

I pick a spot up against the wall. I don't generally go to blues to scam and I don't go to blues to relax or unwind. Sometimes, though, all those things happen by accident. Well, then you gotta take it as it comes, seriously. For me, I do blues sometimes because I can learn all sorts of things, which is what I like to think I try to make my main goal

every second of every day. Every event and incident is a
lesson, it's just people aren't trained to think like that. All of
us, me included—I ain't pointing fingers. We are desensi-
tized to the magic, somehow. When I hear good blues music,
though, I like to just think about what the general deal is
with myself. It's a good time to give myself the State of the
Senses Address. Actually, funny thing, I usually have a separate train of thought for each song, and when the song is
done, the space between the songs, or the applause of the
crowd, breaks me out of it, and the next song projects a
different mood, which gives me a different tint of a color to
dwell on. Tonight, I tell myself I feel free, finally, like, liber-
ated, being out of the apartment, 'cause the walls were closing in on me in the worst way, you gotta understand. I was
wrong trying to sidestep the memory of Leonia, if you've
never been through it, 'cause there's no way you can avoid
doing all the things you once did with the person—you'll go
nuts. We shared every known noun and every little verb—
how can you top that?

So my back's up against the wall, and I'm watching these
guys. It ain't Moe or Slapmeat at all, I see. It's a few white
guys and a black bass player wearing a "GWU" baseball cap,
but don't get me wrong, 'cause they are blasting the blues so
fine and so hard, you wouldn't believe. I mean, last few days,
I've called friends and family, who didn't really do dick for
me, truth be known, but my psychiatrist's check should go to
these guys. The Mulligans. Man, the bass is coating my un-
derbelly 'cause the notes on the bottom are shaking and shining. The drums are over on top of the noise, and slightly
separated, just the way they're supposed to be. The singer
can't sing for shit, in the classical sense, but he's wincing at
all the right notes—no way he can fake that shit, he ain't no

pretty boy. Only virtuoso in the band is the guitar player. But that's okay, we'll excuse him—he probably can't help being talented. Man, I'm a tough motherfucker to please, especially these last few days, but these guys are giving me just what I need. They knew what I needed before I did. These aren't just four guys with instruments; they're a band. They know that cooperating together will make them individually look so much better at the end of the night than each guy trying to do their own thing, however tempting being selfish might be. Man, I think about me and Leonia and how we were two people, an apartment as our arena, playing our separate instruments to our own tempos and on our own private keys, ad libbing lame lyrics as we went along. And if we were a band, we would have been booed off the stage during the opening number, rotten tomatoes sailing towards our snarls from all over the joint.

So, you ever hear that tune "Love in Vain"? Jesus, these Mullies played it slow and mournful, and the clinking of the glasses never took me out of the mood once. Actually, those glasses by the bar were the second percussion, the high hat, and the whole audience seemed part of the band, every minor eruption of laughter was scripted, because it fit so well, happened just when the song needed it. That white boy with the crooked, shit-eating grin and the microphone in his hand closed his eyes and summoned not just his own spirit, not just Robert Johnson's spirit, not just Eric Clapton's baby boy's spirit, but every one of us who have ever loved a woman for an instant longer than she loved us back. And the band was playing, but totally watching him, to see how true he'd be to the music and the lyrics, and he was right on, singing, no, moaning—no, *explaining*—"All my love's in vay-ayn" and the drummer rolled him right out of that phrase like a doctor passing a perfect baby to the mother for the first time.

That's what being in a band means, one there for the other, and all there for the music, the message, the feeling. Who can think or talk if you're listening to someone who feels it? And at that moment, like a lull at a New Year's Eve party, when it goes from bedlam to an eerie silence in an anonymous instant, before some loudmouth punk starts the shit up all over, there was complete silence in the bar—even the sausages were quiet. I wasn't outside so I can't say for sure, but I'd bet anything the cars weren't honking, and the hookers stopped their cursing, 'cause the Mulligans were playing, and that singer was speaking to me, and speaking to us all. It's like all the wheels of the universe hit a snag at just that moment and the axles locked. I don't know if the Mulligans were the cause or just the outcome, but everything was different now. The wheels were turning all different directions, and the vehicle skidded. Skidded, but did not crash. If you can say it like that, out loud, and you let us all be blue with you, then trust me, your love is everything but in vain.

And when the song ended, applause seemed like an insult, so I didn't clap, although I think everyone else did. I just sauntered over to the bar, and ordered—can you guess? The bartender smirked, like I was uttering some kind of bad, pop-blues, whiteboy college cliché, but he just doesn't know me. I mean, he hasn't walked a mile. And I was drinking my drink, and I shuffled a little closer to the bandstand. Why was that first row always empty? Like in a classroom, do only the blues geeks sit in the front row? Well, fuck it, that's the best seat, right? I mean, anyone knows that; don't you want to be where you can see the best? So I shuffled up close, with now half a drink in my glass, and the singer exhaled, and shook his head, like he'd just been through something. He smiled in spite of himself, and looked over at the drummer. The drummer grinned like a kid who got away with something. Had I missed something, maybe a mistake? Shit, where was I? I really have to start paying closer attention to things like that—the little things. But the singer raised his eyebrows, and the drummer slapped his sticks together once and the guitarist bled the opening riff to "The Spider and the Fly," probably my all time favorite. But where's the opening harp? How the fuck can you play that song without harmonica? That's criminal! Holy shit! The bouncer's gonna come get 'em if they play that fucker without harp. So I drain my drink, drop the empty, yank the harmonica out of my ass, and vault up on stage, so it's me and the Mulligans.

I look around, smiling at the crowd—I can't really see individual faces, 'cause the place is so dark, the spotlights all in my eyes. I glance over at the singer who's busy deciding whether or not to slip on a pair of dark sunglasses, really weighing the pros and cons. Lotta concentration there. He eyes me, sort of not committing one way or the other. And I nod over to him, in total good faith. Blues, remember? We share the language.

I grab the microphone and start puffing into it with my harp. Not to brag, but, man, if there's one song I do know, it's "The Spider and the Fly." My, my, my. I'm about nine bars into my opening solo when things get weird and I realize that there's no sound in the air besides my dying breath, some miscellaneous voices, and clinking glasses, even though I know I sounded pretty good. Now, my eyes were clamped shut when I was playing, 'cause I just sort of assumed, on like a leap of faith, that my boys weren't gonna let me down so hard. With the silence and everything, I just don't know what the fuck is going on, so I open my eyes and turn around, only to realize that the drummer is totally through drumming, sticks resting on the drum stand, and the guitarist has let go of the neck of his guitar, allowing the thing to dangle near his dick. The singer, glasses now on, arms folded, his stance—heavier on one foot than the other—indicating that he's kind of pissed, steps back, I think a little afraid. Afraid? Shit, man, hate to tell you, but looks like I miscalculated big time. You gotta know it wasn't supposed to happen like this. The bass player now's just talking to a lady at the side of the stage. Dude! The Mulligans fuckin' stood my ass up! A freeze-out at Terra Blues, man, I didn't think that was possible—I totally missed that one. So I walk over to the guitar player, man, pissed as shit, 'cause now he made me look bad—that just ain't blues etiquette, you know? I'm pointing at him, mad.

"What the fuck, you fuckin' prick, where's my opener?" I'm completely spittin' a whole bunch of leftover whiskey from my mouth to the panels of the stage. Those guys completely hung me out to dry, you have to understand. I was counting on them for just the smallest show of support. I mean, what, do I have to go around tellin' people about the whole Leonia incident? I certainly don't want to spend the rest of my life doing that. And off to the side, I see the singer, glasses now off, waving for the fuckin' bouncer like he's hailing a goddamn cab in the middle of a rain storm. What am I going to do, assassinate the bastard? All I wanted to do was play "The Spider and the Fly" for a while along with them. Have you ever heard of a reaction like this? I turn to the singer.

"What's up your ass, man? You guys too big to jam? You

too big? Let's have a little fun, man, I teach you something, come on!" He smirks at me as the bouncer grabs me by the back of my workshirt with his fingernails all into my neck, and drags my ass off to the side and down the stairs, my hip and head managing to hit the tip of each one. Dante's Inferno was paying a visit to all thirty-three cantos of my brain. It's not only the stairs, but the bouncer is roaring, let me tell you. It's official: I wasn't allowed to do that.

"Had to be a little wiseass? Open mike is on Wednesdays, you little shit, Mr Harmonica Man! Next time think twice about ruining everybody else's good time, you motherfuckin' retard! There're executives and shit tryin' to scout those guys out. How they gonna make it if some shithead like you fucks it up for 'em?" He was spittin' fire, like he didn't like my version of "The Spider and the Fly" much in the least.

So I'm slumped out on Bleecker, back leaning against a brick wall. I can feel Leonia's gun poking into my gut, but it's okay; it's like a little reminder. Right now all that whiskey is coming back to me in waves, and it's not too good now, man, not at all. I can feel it all rise like a tennis ball, solid but rubbery and jumping around inside. If I thought it was like a laser beam going down, now it's like a fireball getting ready to explode into the spray of a thousand brilliant comets. Good God, the only other time I've felt close to this level of shittiness was high school, the night that made me swear off tequila. Long story, kid—trust me. I look up at the bouncer who's still looking over at me, glaring like he wants to kick the shit out of me even more. Have you ever noticed that some people just can't get enough? I turn the other way and puke my guts out for I'd say about three minutes, but I might not be the best judge; there's no way I can say. That's really weird—I don't usually puke. Then again, it's not every day some sausage of a bouncer roughs me up for no reason. Guess it's Trident time, kid. Couples look at each other as they walk around me, giving me a lot of room. Puking's no fun, but I guess the good news is this means at least I won't shit blood the next time around.

I haven't got fucked since Leonia happened. Tonight, it would be nice. To tell you the truth, that was one of the first thoughts that went through my head after the whole thing happened, about the whole sex thing. What, does that make me some kind of common criminal, or something? Probably, but it's the way it is, the way it is for me anyway. Money in the bank for me times like this is one of those little Soho dance clubs, cheap for the cover, and slip in, get a drink or something, and dance to those electronic rhythms. No problem, I can dance. No one complains about me dancing with them, 'cause I can hang all right. I can't dance right now, of course, here on the ground, because I'm closer to dying than to dancing. Dying, dancing, what's the difference? With one you embarrass yourself, and with the other you get judged. So I up and cruise around, both hands free, for the first time all night. No liquor or anything, which is more than okay with me right now. I ball my fist and graze my ass to see if my harmonica is still there. For some reason, it still is. I swear I don't remember anything about putting it in my pocket, 'cause it was the heat of the moment, but I did—I guess that's a sign or something. So I've got my legs back a little, my cards, a little bank, and my harp. Let's dance, kid!

I float past Angelika, check out the cappuccino crowd and the amateur critics leaving the theater. It's fun to hang out on Mercer, see them as they come out of the movie theater, and try to guess what movie they saw. It's easy, man, after you do it for a little while. I'm so good at it, most of the time I can also guess what they ordered at the Angelika Cafe. No problem. Only shitty movies are playing, I can't hang around there for long—subtitles and low budgets—the most self-conscious shit ever. I don't go to movies where I can't pronounce the titles correctly, you know what I mean? What use is that? Who exactly am I trying to impress?

Sapphire's, man, it's really, truly, not a bad club, you gotta believe me. I mean, y'all can go over to Limelight, take all those raves and do what you will with them. Myself, I don't need that shit. I love the hole-in-the-wall joints where I can do what I want, where people dance to dance, not to make it on MTV in their next lives. I'll let you in on a little secret—I dance exactly the same to everything—blues, hip-hop, rock, techno, reggae—I got the same ol' ordinary moves for every kind of music there is. Only thing different is I make sure I'm wearing an expression on my face that goes along with the music, and that usually gets me through anything I can't handle. Actually, I started a slam dance last New Year's Eve—I think we did it to Seal or something. You can slam dance to anything—music is just an excuse, it's practically all in your mood. Sapphire's is somewhere, man, I think definitely past Elizabeth Street, yeah, way past Mott Street, totally East, I think. I'm not too good with street names, but I usually know where I'm going. God, I don't even know the cover for Sapphire's. What's it on Thursdays, three? Four now?

So I slip the biggest guy in New York City four more at the door, and slip in. Not to be a smartass, but I'm kind of happy now that I'm in a place where there isn't live music. Who needs temptation? I make a complete left, as far away from the bar as possible. I think I'll give it a few minutes with the alcohol. Now, clubs like this, believe it or not, when I'm looking to dance with someone, I'm always playing at a little bit of a disadvantage. I'm up against the sausages to-night, and those types of guys have this permanent glazed expression like they're not thinking anything, and they wouldn't mind doing anything. I'm convinced women find that attractive. Women love sausages. Me, I've got some kind of permanent scowl attached to me like a birthmark, and plus my fresh mint Trident is just no match for puke, espe-cially jumpin' Jack puke, believe me. So, it's me versus the sausages, but if I were a betting man, which I sometimes am, I wouldn't pick the sausages.

Yeah, these mechanical songs are blending into one an-other. It's not like the blues, which'll give you verse chorus verse, and maybe, if you're lucky, a bridge once in a while. All dance music gives you are primitive rhythms of violence and lyrics of lust. Good thing I'm in the mood for both. I thrust myself into the exact epicenter of the dance floor, making sure I bump at least three chicks and a couple of male nonentities. It's funny, because I ignore that awkward stage where you go from not dancing to dancing. I just dance, man. Dancing isn't in my blood, but it is on my mind, and I do go for it. It's no problem, because things are good, I guess, and I get through a couple songs quasi-alone. No girls are with me, per se, but I'll say a lot of them are in my vicinity. One sausage steers his kabob of a girlfriend away from me. I take that as a compliment, and drive on. There's this one song blasting out now that I've never heard, that has as a part of it some kind of gimmick when everyone is sup-posed to scream some specific catch phrase. It's about three times before I detect the trend. First of all, I can't figure out when to start screaming—remember, I haven't heard the song before, and second of all, I can't for the life of me figure out what everyone is saying. Also, I'm not Mr Sobriety right now, but you know how that is. I think I have a good ear for lyrics and that kind of thing, but I could swear they're all saying, "Oh, Steroids! Yeah!" And, I mean, I don't think that's too likely. So I'm getting into the groove of it, and who really cares, 'cause it's a crowded place; who's gonna know? And there's a slight rupture in the rhythm, and I feel the chant is coming. So, along with everyone else, tonight's colleagues, I raise my fist and yell out, "Oh, Steroids! Yeah!" as loud as everyone else. I look around, making sure no one realizes that I simply don't know what the hell I'm talking about. I scout around for people laughing at me (here I am, J. Alfred Prufrock on the dance floor, right?) and no one pays me a second, or actually even a first, notice, dude; they're just dancing. Only thing, there's a really petite Asian girl with a big gold heart around her neck and the greatest red plaid hat on her head, backwards. She must have stolen that thing from Holden Caulfield, but I guarantee it looks much, much better on her. She's nodding her head, as if we're grooving to the song together, which I guess by nightclub definition means we are. So I dance, rather than walk—remember this is Sapphire's—my way over to her, and we groove on down. When the crowd participation part comes again, we clasp hands in the air, and both shout our part. I do my very best to yell out one decibel less than her so she can't fully hear me blow my line, and I desperately try to listen up to hear what she's saying, and still, man, it sounds like "Oh, Steroids! Yeah!" Wow, that gets me to thinking that someone might actually have gone ahead and written a song about anabolic steroids. Do weight lifters write dance tunes? That's kind of depressing, but I have no forum to address that now; I'm grooving with Goldheart, and it looks like she's reciprocating the groove. When I dance and I'm with a partner I'm into, I like to dance forever. All through each and every wrinkle of the night, kid. And for some reason, my stomach has never felt better.

"My name is Michelle!" Goldheart just out and out screams into my ear, as if her ass was on fire. And the shape of my skull starts to vibrate and gyrate and shake all around. Boy, my head didn't need that at all. And the whiskey, if some of it isn't sprawled all over the Bleecker Street sidewalk, rises until it fills all the veins in my temples, but what can I do? Shrug it off, make a note: little girl, big voice. But the thing about her name is, I don't care, I never asked, and plus I'm wondering what the hell was so urgent about me knowing it at that exact moment. It's funny how a night out can be going great (not that mine really was, in all honesty) and one little detail can ruin it. So her name is Michelle. So it's Michelle. I look at her, try to smile, and continue to dance. For fuck's sake, the music was loud, but it really wasn't so loud that she had to holler in my fuckin' ear. Now my headache was revving up again in a big way. I don't advise you to have some psycho dragging you down the stairs by your Timberlands and then have some woman start screaming her name in your ear. Damn, man, why did Michelle! have to tell? So I wink at her—charm, man, gotta maintain it at all times—and go to the bathroom. Pseudo-tough guy there, looking pretty shifty-eyed, so I pick the urinal that's closest to him. Ever have one of those nights when you're in the mood for anything? I piss unenthusiastically, all the while looking over at this fidgety little dude with his corduroy Penn State hat askew, the bill pointin' towards the exit. I hadn't seen him out on the dance floor or anything, so the men's room might be his hangout, man, how am I supposed to know?

He catches me starin'. "What, you need something, man?" Ha! His voice sounded just like I thought it would. Unsure. If it sounded sure, I would have bought from him, anything, I guarantee it. It's like an unsteady hand stroking the back of a pit bull. The human knows his own fear, and is trying in total futility to trick the beast. You cannot trick anything until you trick yourself. You gotta convince the animal that he needs what you got, I mean, doesn't everybody know that? Isn't that Lesson One? But, I'm not about to tell this guy, and yet I'm not going to leave just yet either. I mean, let's face it—what's my hurry to get back to Michelle!?

"What's available?" I bet no one talks to him like that. "Available." I can be proud of myself every once in a while, because you could look through thesauruses all night long, and you wouldn't have found a cooler word for that moment. My psycho cousin from Rome tries to speak English sometimes and he says that word "AA (short 'a') VUH (lower than the first syllable) LAY (accent here) BULL (swallow this sound)." It's the strangest sounding word when he says it, but I said it correctly, American-style. See, man, that phrase doesn't come across as being a punk or nothing, but the way I said it, I established that I'm in control, believe it or not, basically because it shows I'm not trying to speak his language. Most people try to talk drug-dealer lingo to him, but then I'm on his terms, and I'm not in control. And who doesn't want to be in control? I admire people who act under control—the bouncer who methodically kicked the shit out of me; Goldheart who waited until what she thought was the right time to tell me what her name was; Leonia. Leonia, she really took control, didn't she?

The Grade-C thug looks around, almost like a cartoon of a gangster, and says, "Buddy, I saw you out there—you need something to get you dancin' like Casanova and MC Hammer and lovin' like a machine gun all rolled into one, right?" He smirks like some men's room Mona Lisa in leather— total angel, man, can't beat it, got to hand it to the guy.

"You got X, huh?" Sounds stupid, right? Like—hey, you can't slip nothing past me. Goldheart is there for me outside, waiting, and I'm humoring some punk. But I know what I'm doing.

"All your troubles, man, up in smoke, no worries. You're my boy, I give you a special deal, come on. No problems. Guaranteed. Wanna feel free as a birdie?" Ooops. He just blew it. Watch this.

"You punk ass motherfucker! Don't even talk to me!" I take him by the back of his collar, just the way the bouncer did to me, shovin' his ass up against the wall. You should have seen my eyes. "Can't you leave me the fuck alone? Nothing you got's gonna do good for nothin' I got." And I look at him, and trust me, I didn't do shit to him, nothin' like what I personally went through before. I summoned the rage. And I acted out of control, but trust me, it was all an act. It was a bluff, but the bluff was enough. I was in even more control than when Goldheart hollered in my ear. But he looked up, and I tasted fear in his eyes, and it wasn't nice at all. It was ugly, and I was instantly sorry he was afraid of me. Deep down inside, maybe it's true, I did want to fight a little bit, but to scrap, not to bully. I guess I just have the habit of picking the wrong sparring partner. Like Leonia, say, I kept waiting for her to fight back. But this punk, I had him ever since I said the word "available." I don't know, man, something about the way I said that. Just knew, I'm telling you. But I straighten out the guy's collar of his gorgeous black leather jacket (wonder where he got the money), give him a little look and try to find the girl. God, X-Man in the bathroom knew not what he was getting into. I mean, he deserved it—he was offering me an ancient cure for a brand new disease.

I go back to Michelle!, and she seems to have gotten yet a little nuttier. What, did she have another drink or something while I was gone? She motions over to me, and the Incredible East Village Red Sea of Sausages parts, and it's all me. We dance forever, wearing out the repertoire of the DJ, surviving new sets of crowds, seeing new sausages, but we all know sausages are the anti-snowflake—no two of them are different. And through all the records and songs, all the different decades that came through the speakers, that girl and me are learning about each other as we're learning each other's moves. I'm doing my best to be an unpredictable dancer, but unless she's X'd up herself, she knows what's behind my gilded dance steps. I wish I could look you in the eyes and tell you the truth about our dancing: it is a damn good time, really good, great connection. Yeah, a great time, although I'm half-expecting, half-looking forward to X-Man's inevitable switchblade to cut through the back of my own workshirt. You could tell straight off he'd be the back-stabbing type, if anything. A warning: yo, if anyone tries to attack me, they had better be ready to kill me, because I'm much more prepared to die than to live tonight. I'm also much closer. I guess when it all comes down to it, you have to be ready to die before you're ready to live. Yet another reason I admire pretty Leonia; yet another reason why I can't shake the vision. So the strobes from the ceiling are wrestling with all the precious metals around her neck. It looks nice tonight. And we dance, and for some reason the DJ (remember, it's getting so late it's *early,* you know where I'm coming from?) flips on a slow one—I didn't know that was possible at Sapphire's, to be honest, it's got to be a first—and Michelle somehow calms down, and we again clasp hands, jigsaw-puzzle city, and they fit just right, mine only a little bigger than hers, just the way you want it. We sway a little bit, she moves gradually, and I am her shadow, her echo, the image in the mirror she sees every day. I stare down at her hips, and when she sees that she shakes them like a vamp, and we both look up, laughing ridiculously. Did you catch that? I think that's the first time I laughed in maybe a month. And it's the first time I meant it in forever. I don't know how to describe it, but it was funny; maybe you just had to be there. Life's funny, but you have to *be* there to truly get it; there's just no way to explain it all. And she closes her eyes in this cartoonish blend of seduction and wasted delirium and she screams out of nowhere, to the music in some corner of her memory (swear to God, kid), "Oh, Steroids! Yeah!"

Now, I don't know if she came with a sausage or any other friends or anything, but when she left, she left just with me, I can tell you that. I mean, I checked behind me a few times, believe me. There was a break in the music for a while, and I heard everyone hustling around, saying all the things they would have said before, but the music was too loud. And I was still holding her hand, which felt great—that's true with pretty much all Asian women's hands, something about them, they got the feel of a big time connection—and I kind of buoy her up for a while as she leads me out, letting her bare legs lead the way. Hell, I got nowhere in mind. Sapphire's man, it gets crowded on weekends, but it always manages to work for me. And it stays open forever.

I check out the feel outside, and it's misting, with all the invisible droplets hitting me. I look at the profile of Michelle with the gold heart buried in her jacket, and everything slips right into place. Told you I'd beat those fuckin' sausages. All I can determine is that it's well into the morning, no doubt about that. So Goldheart and I walk for two blocks, tops, and she drags me into the lobby of this kind of excellent apartment building, with mirrors all around, as high up as the ceiling. I'm not sure if I needed to see me in all those mirrors, but then again, it's not like I had a choice or anything, the chick picked the place, you know; maybe it's her place. And so we drag each other up a few steps, and then she makes a tiny fist out of her hand, and punches the up button for the elevator. Hard. I don't know why she does that, but she must be feeling something. That last slow song, man, the melody is still going around in my head, not leaving me for anything. I don't know who the tune is by, and I can't even remember one word in the entire thing, or else I might go as far as to treat myself to the single. I wonder if Goldheart remembers it. I graze my ass—harp still there, you know it. So after the girl hits, and I mean hits, the black button, she collapses and starts laughing, she sits down right there on the ground, right in the middle of the lobby, and it's a nice building and everything, and who knows when people will start leaving their apartments—I just couldn't tell you what time it is. Then she looks at me and slaps the ground next to her, and I sit down. I don't care, what do I got to lose? So I'm basically looking all over the place, sort of curious to see if other people are around, or what the scene is. I'm not the type that's into people seeing me do stuff, you know? Man, I'm telling you, I couldn't even begin to *guess* what time it is, give or take three hours. If someone asked me the time I would have said: gettin' light, already. I just have no idea, man.

And while I'm thinking that, she starts kissing me with the softest, smallest lips around my neck. Like the mist. I don't even ordinarily go too much for that neck shit, but this girl has definitely got something. Something about strange lips against my face gets me every time—that's probably a problem. She manages to kiss me like some sort of lovely Asian mosquito or something; it's like she kisses me maybe fifty times in like six seconds. How that drunken mouth can move like the fuckin' wings of a hummingbird, I'll never know, but it does feel nice, I can tell you that. After x minutes of her doing that, she does her best imitation of a sober girl, and whirls around and hits the up button again, only softer this time. The doors open and she does her best to haul me inside. I topple over her (okay, maybe I did it just for effect) and she goes crashing to the floor, and we are tangled in one big mess of transcontinental lust on the floor of this fine elevator, which I now see also has mirrors on the walls and mirrors on the ceiling, and shiny-ass wood on the bottom. Mahogany? She puts her fingers underneath my workshirt and up into my chest. Get this, no shit, she then looks up at my face, *impressed*. I have no idea why, I'm no athlete, I don't lift, and my chest is nothing great, trust me. I shrug. "Oh, Steroids." Now don't laugh—it was on my mind, so I just said the shit. And she bought it, I guess.

Now, like I've been telling you, I have no sense of time,

and I have no concept of details or anything, but we didn't make love right away, just then, but we just kind of smothered each other for a while, doin' shit, and at one point the door opened, though there weren't any people there, I don't think. When the doors opened, we made our way out and into a stairwell. Girl like that, she didn't think to wonder that I insisted on taking my black jeans off myself—yeah, that's just what I need, another crazy girl touching the fuckin' gun. So we did a little of everything. We didn't talk too much during it, but I hoped the whole time that she was tasting the Trident and not the puke, I mean that's my idea of urban chivalry. It was more fun to watch her come than anything I've ever seen in my few years on this planet. I looked up from beneath her body, her thin eyes closed in a pained perfection. It was like she worked herself up to it, happily constructing her own mini-apocalypse. All the shit her face went through, it would be weird for onlookers who didn't know better to understand that I was actually being good to her, doing her a favor, in a sense. But it was nice, really; I just can't help breakin' a little chops. After a while she fell asleep, and I just laid back against the fire hose. I mean, girls like that, they can make you so sad. This girl was so gorgeous, in the nicest way, totally positive. I would have taken her to my parents if the circumstances were a little different. I could have been with her forever, and at the same time, it was shameful that I was there even for that little spittle of time. I'm no hippie and I'm no stalker or psycho, but it's always been my philosophy that if you're going to go to bed, and you have the choice, you might as well be next to the most attractive woman you can find. And I was. And who's laughin' now, between me and those sausages, man, 'cause they went home and banged their heads together or did more shots or something, for fun, and the next day they all can talk about how cool Sapphire's is, and how hot all the chicks were, and how one of 'em was "coming on to me," et fuckin' cetera: means nothin'.

So Goldheart is resting in my arms, and the laziest, sloppiest, most amorphous dream of all time slips into my head, with my head resting against a fire hose. I'm awake enough to know I'm dreaming, and I'm asleep enough to know Leonia's dead and gone, to know that each second I don't think about her, she just gets deader, and people like Goldheart get more alive. Those mingling frat boys at Sapphire's, the bouncer at Terra, even, are more alive than Leonia. My last thought before I finally surrender to sleep's narcotic is that everyone in my life does favors for me, things that will certainly benefit me in the long run, and what do I really do for them? I mean, do I even give them a single thing? Everyone seems to be on this planet for me, even strangers: the bouncer, my parents, X-Man in the bathroom, Leonia, certainly Goldheart, and even the guys from the Mulligans. That's a very uncomfortable thought, man, 'cause don't I owe them something? Damn, that's not too pleasant to think about. But, I mean, that singer, I mean, was I off key? Doesn't he like music?

And the dream fuses with the dreamscape, and I'm thinking now only of Michelle. I want it to remain concrete, all those kisses on my neck. I wish I had counted them! When she felt my chest, and then looked up at my face, why didn't I have my camera? Oh, God, why didn't I keep track of all my fights with Leonia, write down the transcripts like some fuckin' talk show or court case? What was I thinking about instead? Where was my head? Do I need dance lessons? Do I need, after all, harmonica lessons? I need a toothbrush, a paintbrush, a hairbrush, anything to make Goldheart not regret falling asleep in my arms, man, don't you see? I want to be there for her, not forever, but just for tonight and through the morning, just with the fire hose, and just so that she'll never think of Sapphire's or necks or that steroids song or elevators without thinking of me. And what does it mean if I can go on to other people so smoothly after less than a week's time, a bottle of Jack Daniels whiskey and a slow dance? And what does it mean if I do decide to go to open mike on Wednesday? And what does it mean, if now when I wake up in some New York City stairwell, I think not of Leonia or of music, or of myself, and I don't care if I left Leonia's gun or the harmonica someplace, but I wake up, and sit up, and open my eyes for them to glow like twin moons, for them to shine like Vatican visions, and I think of something that I never have before. The new detail. But what does it mean? I want to be able to terrorize my opponents, only thing I don't seem to even know how to identify them. I don't want to wake up with more questions than I had when I fell asleep. I don't want to go to bed tired and wake up exhausted. I want to have something specific on my mind, you know. I want a motherfuckin' purpose. I want a living, breathing agenda like a suit or a sausage. If I had a wish right now, if I could hit up some street-corner genie to grant me anything I wanted, I would ask for only one thing, kid. I want to wake up screaming. Screaming something specific. Screaming a name. Screaming, *"Michelle!"*

I have no way of knowing this, but it occurred to me that we were, or at least I was, closer to coma than just sleep. I don't know, but I had too many dreams and too many thoughts for it to have just been my usual few hours. For me, I haven't slept at all since Leonia did herself in—all those relentless ghosts in my apartment shakin' my shoulders whenever I approached the kingdom of sleep, I guess— what's your excuse, Goldheart? I like poetry as much as the next guy, and it was total fuckin' poetry that I woke up before Michelle did, and kissed her right there on the neck. Instead of going nuts like she did, I put my lips together, and rested them on her throat, and when I released them it made the softest little mini-suction sound, and it was all right. I waited for it to echo through the cavernous stairwell of the apartment building, but it did not. Not knowing what floor I was on, I just started walking down the stairs, and it was quite a few flights before I made it outside, in the middle of the rain, onto the sidewalks of Houston Street, and back into the depth of another dying day and those thick memories of Leonia and the way she left.

Like the whiskey that my body refused to accept (and I don't really blame it), it was impossible to digest my recent history, and certainly impossible to even think about what I was going to do in the future. That word—*future*—could be the fuckin' punch line to the joke that is my current existence. Don't even say that word around me, man, it couldn't be any more meaningless. In my own way, I tried to honor music and art when I got on the stage at Terra, only to be thrown off and bruised. So maybe gettin' thrown out was art in and of itself? Yeah, that makes me feel better to think of it in that way. It really does. But I just wanted to play. I wanted to succeed, to come out from under the shadow of the bullet. But it won't work, because Leonia made sure she got the last fuckin' word, didn't she? The gunshot was like a door slamming, and then the dead bolt. So what's left to say?

Who knows, but before I get myself killed, I should probably get myself on the night bus home. I'm in no hurry, buses leave pretty much all night long, and I don't especially want my parents to be up when I show. The 'rents, man, you should see 'em. They're asleep before ten, and then up before the crack of dawn with pots clanging. I guarantee they'll be tucked away when I get home, and here's hoping they'll just roll over, have some mercy, and leave the hellos until the morning. No chance of a totally clean entrance, because the old dog, Clamor, barks like nuts whenever there's so much as a mouse farting on our property. That's his job. I named him, in case you were wondering. Port Authority isn't that bad a walk, but I'm not really the biggest buff when it comes to sightseeing, if you haven't guessed. But I do kind of like the Hudson, in a weird kind of way. I know this is crazy, but I happen to think the George Washington Bridge came before the Hudson River, like the bridge is older, even though that doesn't seem possible at all. Just tellin' you how it seems. Going home, somehow, is like a defeat in the worst way. You don't go home; you retreat home. There's nothing, and I mean nothing, glorious or victorious about visiting your parents at your old house. Parents? God, I mean my parents don't know Michelle, they never met her, man; they don't even know I can play the harmonica. And I can play the fuckin' harmonica—Terra Blues is not a true indication, that was just some bouncer. And I'm slugging my way up Eighth Avenue. To tell you the truth, I'm in no hurry to be where I am and I'm in no hurry to get where I'm going. In any case, I pray for the first time since Leonia left. I pray, falling to pieces, telling God, wherever He may be, thank You, dear God; thank You so much for putting the Port Authority over here on the West Side, close to the sunset.

You know how it is, sometimes you love to go for a walk or something, and notice new things: "Oh, I never knew that old oak tree had that little nook in there, man, and look, what a strange pattern on the bark," or, "Jeez, did you ever notice the deli over there has a bullet-hole in the window?" you know, shit like that. I'll admit, sometimes I'm like that. Who doesn't like to discover new things? But today, up Eighth Avenue, man, all I'm thinking about is getting to the Port. That's it. And I've seen all these stores before; I've seen all the crazy people threatening other crazy people. I've seen all the cops' dirty looks before. You may not understand, but I guess now I have a different set of priorities. Let's face facts—my girlfriend killed herself. You know what that means? Me neither, but let's say it's kind of hard to get excited about a tree or something like that so soon after. So I put it on cruise control and let my feet do the walking and my brain do the wandering. That's okay, because dusk has given way to darkness, and I'm walkin' slow. Oh, usually, when there's a Don't Walk sign, I walk anyway and dodge. Not now. Hey, man, the sign says Don't Walk, what am I gonna do? So I don't walk, deferring instead to the stationary darkness. Can't remember the last time I ate, but that's okay; there'll be something at home. But traveling, like religion, or a funhouse mirror, I've noticed, allows for awful reflection.

It's a crowded night, people are hustling home, and I swear I see Leonia appear across the street. I know instantly it can only be *her* fingerprint of a silhouette, with the frill of her coat and her mountain of hair. Her old lady posture, her poet's laugh. The music of her being, the sadness of her music. The spirit and energy of her sadness. I'm so mad at Leonia. What she did, man, she did to *me*. The bullet went through the roof of her mouth, by way of my heart. And her body crumpled, and the blood soaked the linoleum, overflowing the space between the tiles, so explain this to me: how did she look as beautiful as ever? Explain to me how she was a vision in death, explain to me how that idiotic death pose was somehow synonymous with her falling asleep on the couch on a Sunday while reading the sports section— how's that, man? Tell me how I looked at the blood get fainter and fainter the farther it was from her body, and the parts of the stream that made it to the kitchen looked like when someone tries to finish writing a sentence when their pen is running out of ink. And when you write your autobiography and your epitaph is in blood, it doesn't have to rhyme; it's already poetry. But across the street, I mean, that can't be Leonia's exact silhouette, right? That can't be hers at all. I let the shade move on, it's probably someone harmless, I ain't gonna hassle her. I'm wary enough about talking to the living, but there's this whole thing about contacting the dead, you know? I wouldn't even try that—I don't think Leonia would want to hear what I have to say. I am so mad at Leonia. Yeah, just what I need—to go through all that trouble and all those mysterious dimensions to contact Leonia, just to tell her that I think she's nothing but a quitter.

Still on auto pilot, I'm up to Gate 220 I know the Port better than the damn custodians, probably. I don't take the escalator steps two at a time, like usual. Shit, if I have to wait, I have to wait—no one's expecting me or anything. The Port is fuckin' crawling with the living dead at night— all the animals come out at night. No problem, you just gotta become one. Lucky for me at this point I don't have too far to go, and no one looks twice at me. A lot of people are hustling around, and I ease my way up there. I wait for fuckin' ever, easily more than an hour, until the bus I need pulls up. Must mean one just pulled out as I came into the gate. Two people are behind me in line for the bus. Some couple with about twenty bags. It takes them like five minutes just to board. I don't offer to help. I just sit down in the back. I can't help but think that this terminal is the worst kind of dungeon—fumes and subhumans, and cursing and plagues and people rushing around for no good reason I mean whatso-fuckin'-ever. My eyes meet the bus driver's in that crazy long horizontal rearview. Did he just give me a dirty look? Is he nuts? So I give him a night-bus-home smile—pained, like my front teeth are clamped down on a thick piece of rope. Fuck you, bussie, shove your attitude, and stand on the motherfuckin' gas and take me home. Trust me, you have no idea, you haven't walked a mile in mine, ma'. I settle down by the window and just stare out. The doors creak wildly and the exhaust gasps, and the dinosaur lurches forward, angry, finally ready to attack the night.

I did a lot of things wrong, man, I mean *a lot*. I'm not even talking about the deadly sins, or a lot of things that should be sins but aren't. I fucked up a lot along the way, you just can't imagine how much. I hope I'm not trying to paint myself as no superhero—I got flaws the size of my jaws, kid. Made some big, big mistakes. I gotta see me now, right now—where's my face? I remember the mirror on the ceiling of Goldheart's elevator, and I remember the mirror in the bathroom of my apartment, where Leonia used to look at herself and critique out loud. People smile for mirrors, man, they pose. You're not looking at yourself; you're looking at the best case scenario of yourself. Fuck that! I move my face back, like, six inches from the window dividing the night from myself. The light frames me in silver and black, and it works as a mirror of my own. I lock in on myself, can't look away. Won't. I'm in a stare down with myself, and as the bus books, the sights of New York City are orbiting my face, scowling, man, always scowling, as the dinosaur tumbles even faster, and it's bumpin', but I ain't movin' my eyes from my eyes. I somehow increase my concentration to that next level, like a trance or something, and I become the face in the reflection, starin' at myself starin' at myself. God, the mistakes! I made so many mistakes! Who's gonna blink first, punk? Not me. I'm not moving, kid, I ain't even thinking about moving, kid! And the scarier it gets, the more my past filled with flaws swarms around my eyes, the meaner my face gets—my left eye inflates, my eyebrow slants, my lips part slightly in defiance of the cosmos and the dead; and the lamp posts and storefronts let me be—they don't have my attention, or respect, and do you know what? They know it! Oh, God, I'm staring at myself and my mistakes are hovering over me, it's like I can see my feebleness in every speck of matter in the bricks of the stores and every fraction of fire in the corrupt stars, and I don't think the mistakes will ever go away, definitely not tonight. I gotta stare 'em down, though, gotta be tough, gotta hang together, gotta be the master of darkness.

My eye is set on the image of my eye, reversed, and I can only assume that my harmonica is somewhere. I can only assume the gun is tucked. I can only assume that Goldheart is waking up somewhere with a Leviathan hangover, and she feels happy about me. I can only assume that the bouncer at Terra and that strange singer (I only wanted to jam, have some fun, you gotta understand that above all else) feel some pang, some shard of the guilt that I do. Shard, man, that's all I'm askin'. Did Leonia have time to feel guilty while the bullet was in flight? Mistakes, man, haunting my ass. Inadequacy, mediocrity, haunting my lonely ass. But my mind, I learn, is only moving, operating, progressing, as long as my head is still. Completely still. So I ain't blinking until I get home. That's the only way. When you stare down memories, mistakes, guilt, if you blink, you're dead, motherfucker. And every now and then, blinding streaks of light shoot from the street to my eyes, and my whole face twitches, but I told you already, I'm still. I ain't blinking, kid. Lights erupt as I get closer to home. Look there, a bumbling vagrant with a stogie who stumbles. The night unfolds, and the world comes out from undercover. Mistakes. Shit. Mistakes? I never, never, never should have told her I loved her.

THE PRODIGAL SON

My parents live on the corner of a dead-end street on the outskirts of a dead-end town, at the Eastern tip of a dead-end world. And yeah, I'll be the first to admit, in a way being a little kid on the dead-end was good, because you could play around in the street without cars whizzing by or honking or hittin' people, or anything like that, but looking back years later with a little objectivity, I think maybe I needed to see some cars, some traffic. You know what I mean? Just some sort of reminder that somebody, somewhere was going someplace else to do something, anything. This town, its people have always been content, and that's a good trait for some people to have, but it certainly shouldn't be a kid's goal when he's eleven. I mean, what happens to the kids in town who don't want to be told that everything is better than they know it really is? Kids, by nature, should not be content— they should be forever striving, until life finally kicks them around a little and sends 'em crying back home.

Human beings should want to conquer the world until it's proven that they can't. Me, man, I got all the proof I need. Case closed, kid. You won't hear any argument from me. Some of my friends, they picked colleges and jobs as far away from this town as possible, so they make sure they never visit at Thanksgiving, stuff like that. Another buddy of mine, he works down at the local fire department, still living with his folks, same house he did when he used to get spankings and allowances. And he's probably as content as he ever wants to be. But traffic, at least traffic would have told me that people and places exist beyond my sight. It's like the whole thing about object permanence, where a small child learns that even when he can't see something with his own two eyes it can still exist. I was probably eighteen before I developed that on a global level, you know? I mean, what do I know about farms, things outside of my hometown? But now I don't need to smell the manure to know that that kind of life is real, at least as real as my own. I know it may not be in people's best interest for you to realize this, but there's a world out there, man, information for you to learn. That's important to know, important to keep in mind. But traffic in my head, traffic in the streets, traffic in the sky, all that leads to thoughts, thoughts spilling sloppily until they overflow the labyrinth inside my skull.

Take New York City, man; to me, it's all about movement. That's what New York City means to me, constant motion, constant quest for motion, like a shark, or you're dead. And this place here is *Comaville*. I mean, I figured out the slogan a long time ago: do it, but do it quietly; go ahead and order it, but order a medium; ask, but ask nicely. Moderation, anonymity, and son, mind your manners.

You know what used to get me up out of bed when I lived home? The front door slamming. Weekends and stuff, I could feel it, feel it so deep inside when my 'rents were getting ready to leave, hear them pacing around looking for that last thing or item that they could never find, hear 'em take Clamor out one last time, hear the harmony of their key chains. Man, and I was *itchin'* to get up out of bed, 'cause I had been up thinking, maybe reading, for such a long time, hours sometimes, but who wants to small talk the 'rents first thing in the morning? Please! So they'd keep forgetting shit and doubling back, and I'd be in my bed pushing 'em out of the house with whatever kind of mystical power I had or could invent; I'd be pushing. And Ma would stay back an extra second to scratch Clamor, or toss him a racquetball, or something—let's face it—pretty unnecessary. And Dad would remember a stamp, or something that could clearly wait 'til later. But then you'd hear their footsteps get a little more forceful, like they made up their mind, and the door would groan open with Dad's tug—like a wisdom tooth comin' out, that bastard of a door, ever since I was young— and they'd leave and, good God almighty, would they slam that door. The boom, and I'd be up, kid!

So, look how much time has passed and I'm still playin' the same game. Only thing, the 'rents are not, because they are waiting around for me to get up which means they wanna talk, wanna check up on me, wanna make sure every-thing's peachy, wanna bring up the L-word, even, so they can say they did their part, and we all can just move on. Wouldn't that be nice? So I figure this stuff out, and I'm not ready for it all just yet. I force myself to go back to sleep, really concentrate on it. Well, now, I think it's fairly obvious that that's not the best way to sleep—who wants to have to make an effort to relax? That's no way to lead a life, you know? Anybody knows that forced dreams when you're asleep are just as bad as forced dreams when you're awake. So I can't help it, but I slip into a ruptured dream about closets and caves and cages and graves, with no lead on what

the fuck they have to do with me. Dude, if you can send me
a book on Jung, I'd read it cover to cover and give it right
back to you, same night. I'm talkin' one sitting, 'cause my
curiosity is up there. Caves? What the hell do I look like, a
damn spelunker? Well do I? Who knows, I can't say, maybe
I do lately.

But even trying works, I guess, because the day flickers to
amber, and I hopscotch from an apparently imagined cave to
an assumed legitimate bed. And the smell of Mom's split-pea
soup doesn't waft or float. It fuckin' kicks my door down,
stomps across my room, rippin' up floor boards as it goes.
And don't fuckin' knock Ma's split-pea. I know you must be
wondering why my mom would just toss on some Joe
Schmoe soup for the prodigal son, but it ain't about that. I
dare you to try to completely finish one bowl of my ma's
soup. I don't know what she does to it, what she puts in the
shit, how she cooks it or anything, but all I know is you can
eat it, and what you don't finish (and you won't finish it all,
trust me) you can caulk the ceiling or pave the driveway
with. But boy, does it go down smooth. And no bacon or
prosciutto in there, man, no way; that ain't what split-pea is
about. So the smell is reminding me that it's been days since
I ate—all I had was the Daniels, and that's all gone now,
here's hoping.

Yeah, I need that soup, and I mean, it smells just about
ready to me. I'll tell you straight off, not to say they're perfect, by any stretch, but I'm not going to sit around harshin'
on my parents. They asked me home, no one else is gonna
take me in, and I wanted to see 'em, I guess. What I been
through, I'm glad to wake up in my old bed. The weird
thing is that of course this pillow feels like home, but somehow so too did the fire hose I woke up against the day

before. And the mattress in some way manages to be synonymous with Goldheart and the way when I woke up, I saw
we were in a tight knot, peaceful twins of difference. Besides
telling you it's a feeling of belonging, of miraculously being
in the right place at the right time, all I can say is that it's
something I haven't felt much in my life at all, for sure
recently. Basically, it's something I can't explain to you all
that well. And even if I could, I guess I'm just not going to
right now. I'm not always the type to just go ahead and
define things.

The split-pea smell just grabs a hold of me and lifts me
up by the collar, same one the bouncer at Terra kind of
ruined, if you look at it close enough. It gets me vertical, on
my Timberlands, which are still on. The floor creaks like
crazy when I finally get up from bed, so when I walk down
the stairs of the attic, my room, to the hallway, the fuckin'
welcoming committee is already at the bottom—everybody,
even my sister, the actress. I mean, my mom and dad and
sister are looking at me like I'm going to pull out a gun and
commit a fuckin' family-a-cide, pet-a-cide, and then a suicide. How ridiculous. I do know I look like shit, and I'm
sure I smell like blood, like sweat, like dirt—probably like
an orgasm, too, come to think of it. That wine-red workshirt, for the first time, suddenly feels sloppy. The spring is
out of my step, the trash is out of my talk. With each stride
down the stairs, I lose the pain of adulthood and even the
vestige of personal tragedy, and I am smothered by the familiar confusion of a kid. I become eight again. I imagine
Michelle, with the gold heart teasing gravity, seeing me now,
seeing me inferior and inadequate, seeing me hug my ma,
kiss my sister on the cheek—she just stood there, Isabel, and
took it like a vaccination—and shake my dad's hand. You

think Michelle would recognize me like this? It really matters to me that she remembers me, I wish I could sit you down and explain it to you, about that Michelle. That whole thing meant something to me, and it wasn't the Daniels tricking me at all; it was the time, the place, the person, the fact that I transcended the sausages, maybe, but I would put money on it, man, I meant something to her, too. So I look into my dad's eyes, and he looks a little confused, like an actor on stage who has forgotten his lines. You ever see that shit? When an actor moves from being an actual character to just an ordinary actor in a split second—it takes you right out of the mood, man, talkin' refund city, kid, can't listen to another word of it. And my dad does his best to suppress the panic. Like I said, I didn't bother to write the script, that kind of shit ain't worth it. Let's ad lib, Pops. And I lead my family into the dining room to eat dinner.

"Dear Lord, thank you for the blessings you have given us today. Thank you, Lord, for the food we are about to eat, for allowing us to be together as a family, and for seeing us through in this, our hour of greatest need." My pop has a thick Italian accent, and it's the real thing. He looks up at Mom with his, "how did I do?" look. As in, "that was what we discussed, right?" Imagine an actor who in one scene has forgotten his lines, man, I mean, blown them to high heaven, and then has to come back out on stage the next scene and deliver some soliloquy that's supposed to rock your world, that's supposed to move you, that's supposed to send a message. Impossible. Ah, there I go again, no need to point that kind of shit out, man, he's just my pops. What am I gonna do, sit around and complain about things? Grace was a nice gesture, though—apparently reserved for Thanksgiving, Christmas, and when one of his kids' roommates kills themselves. I'll make a note. Damn, Isabel is looking at me like I'm stirring up my soup with my dick instead of the spoon. Not a bad idea; I should have thought of that years ago if I wanted some big-time attention. If you want attention, though, suicide takes the cake, trust me on that, but it's so blatant, such an obvious "look at me," that it just ends up being bad form. Oh, but at the dinner table? Yeah, kid, should have whipped my dick out when I was nine instead of spillin' milk on purpose, which I did do. I do confess, I do confess, my man, but let's face it—a beating is better than a freeze-out any day of the week. Ask anyone. My folks, though, hearts of gold, but they're all afraid they're going to say the wrong thing, and I guess, so am I (afraid that they're going to say the wrong thing). So if you don't know what to say, what, you're just supposed to be quiet, right? "Amen."

"Pass the soup," I say. Fuck it, I'm hungry. Six desperate claws try to be the one to pass it to me. Whatever. I can't control people, make 'em think things are the way they really are. I plunge the spoon into the green abyss, piercing this weird, leathery lining at the top. I never could understand that, from a purely scientific point of view. I mean, that can't be all that healthy. I lower my face to the edge of the bowl and flip it right in my mouth. The lights go on, my body roars to a start, and my survival instinct finally kicks in. I feel warm, so warm; I sit up straighter. My eyes can focus, and they smile. "The best, Ma, split-pea is the best."

So Isabel starts makin' small talk about things in her high school, and Mom picks up on the easy opportunity and goes off, and they just start blabbing. Supposedly Izzy is going to be the big star in her high school's production of *Romeo and Juliet*. Letting kids like that act is just a bad idea. They're too young, man—I'm telling you. What you're doing is training them to be someone else before they know how to be themselves. Like with the window on the bus home, I try to literally move my face back from the conversation a few inches, and it works. Now, like when you're studying with the tube on, the people become background music, and I can concentrate on the soup, concentrate on my thoughts. All I have to do is work up a little smirk every few minutes, which I do, and then everything is cool. I mean, it's been decades' worth of this, man, I mean, with my family avoiding the central issue at hand. People saying this and meaning that, leaving it to you to figure out what the whole deal is. I was stuck trying to make heads or tails of situations when I was six, if you can believe that. Tell me, what does it mean when a family is shy around each other, around themselves? Lotta that shit, ego shit, whatnot, comes back to haunt kids in the worst way. Especially sensitive ones. I'm telling you the truth on that one; you gotta trust me on that. So depressing, looking at 'em all trying, trying, trying to be a family when there's no real need, in my opinion. Let's just talk about it, man. Let's just talk about anything, anything that's *real*. I don't need a minister or a psychiatrist, or even a blues band—I just need to know my family likes me more than I like myself, which isn't a whole lot right now. Also, I just need a little time. The question is, good Lord, maybe You can answer this, am I gonna get some time, or what?

"But being an actress is probably the most tasking job there is," Isabel explains to Mom, a former actress. "You're attempting to duplicate the flow of consciousness while lining that with subliminal and subconscious interpretation. That's why shows that mock the acting process, shows with laugh tracks and jingles, piss me off so much." I mean Isabel

NAME THE BABY

is talkin' like those Meet the Press punks, arms waving, crazy intellectual expression on her face. My little sister, the one that used to puke on me nightly when she was a baby, suddenly up and became some kind of dramatic theorist. Not what I need in my life, I can say that up front. Kid, be a kid. Damn, my family, do you hear 'em? I've either gotta spend less energy on their conversation or more, but things don't seem right the way they are. Jeez, you leave your sister for a year or so and she turns into one of those. One-a-those, motherfucker. I'll tell you stories, man, people date her and stuff, and I just don't go for it—they just make her mad, they make her mean, and I mean, I just want her to stay the way she is, or I guess go back to the way she was. I hope we get a chance to talk about things. I'd love it if something could stay sacred around here, if it isn't too late. I also might even humor her and ask her about this philosophy of hers. Did I hear that correctly? Was she actually trying to psycho-analyze the role of the thespian? A lotta gall. Sounded suspiciously like bullshit to me. No reason she should be doing that out loud. Sad thing is, if I heard a strange girl say that at a party, I'd probably try to tap her. And I probably would do all right, if you'd be betting—I know just what to say to those kinds of people. See, the best thing you can say about people like that is that they're not just kabobs. Let's face it, those artsy types are a fraud but at least they're not harmful (harmful to themselves and sometimes others like those damn sausages are, I'm convinced). But Clamor happens to save me, starts givin' me the "can you believe the shit I put up with 24–7" look, and I know he's feeling the same thing I am—suffocation! I'm up and I tell the 'rents and Izzy I'm taking my thunderpup for a walk, and they all gasp cartoon

sighs of relief that cause the flames on the unnecessary can-
dles on the table to bend over all the way backwards,
splintering the spines of the fire for good.

I've taken Clamor for a million walks, and not to be
boring, but we always pretty much adhere to one particular
route. Now's a great time because it's fuckin' *dark;* I mean
black-dark, not just absence-of-light-dark, and I can just let
my mind go wherever it wants to go at that moment. I mean,
Clamor doesn't give a fuck—he doesn't want me to small
talk him or pander to him. What attention does he need?
He'll take the attention if you want to give it, sure, but he's
got thoughts of his own that he can sort out on the walk.
And he's a German Shepherd, so the boy just does not get
tired. He loves to be with me, to tell you the truth. But he
takes after me a lot, or, gotta admit, maybe I patterned him
in my own image a bit. His silver link chain is danglin' and
jinglin', singing the song of intimidation and warning to all
the bitches in the 'hood. We had him neutered, but I don't
think it worked—his mojo is working overtime as it is. And
see, with Clamor, it's always been that I'm walking along in
the summer, shirt off, tanned, feelin' good about myself, but
the girls in town won't give me the time, no, they'll just walk
right up on by me, stoop on down and give my *dog* a kiss and
a scratch, and then be on their way. And what's with me?
Not a glance, lady-lady? And the worst part of it is that my
boy will look at me with a sloppy grin on his face, makin' me
feel real stupid. I'd always heard dogs were color blind, but
still, I know he could always tell when I blushed. But I'm
over that, I mean, why feel inadequate over nothing, that's
my stance. Hey, as long as we both know he's better looking
than me, who really gets hurt?

And Clamor and I pierce the skin of the darkness with

our bad intentions. I can hold my own, you know that, and Clamor sure can, too, but something about attacking the town as a tandem makes both of us walk with more of a strut. I'm not saying this town is too dangerous or any-thing—my parents wouldn't want to live in one that was too bad—but if you know what's good for you, you're still gonna look over your shoulder every now and then at night. That's only smart, buddy. We can be frank about this: no one's gonna do shit to me in this town, but I still need my boy at my side—not necessarily for protection, but to make me real, to make me complete. Every now and then a car screams around the curve, but that's no problem—Clamor and I just veer over to the curb, we don't break stride or concentration. And the images of the night turn familiar, and the stones on the street compromise their shapes, and the glory moon in high heaven splits and scatters, and the stars in the sky are spread for all seasons. Is it selfish to think all those things are only there for you? Is it selfish to think that no one else is looking at the stars at that instant, and that they're just put-ting on a show for you, so you can have an inside joke, a secret, among just you two? And, of course, shortly, the phe-nomenal theater of the universe fades, and I imagine Leonia, with her grace of a diamond, until I showed on the scene and interrupted, stomping my Timberlands to the wrong rhythm, tripping her up in the process. Only way for me to look at it is that life got in the way of love, and death got in the way of life, restoring the love.

Clamor stops short, like a typical beast of burden. I don't even bother to look at what he's fussin' over (now *that's* selfish, my man), figuring it's some kind of squirrel, or some-thing else he thinks is the biggest deal in the world. Dogs have weird-ass priorities; if you have one, I'm sure you know that already. Bottom line, though, is that we're on the walk together, and if he needs to stop, that's good enough for me. I tug him, just to check if he'll lose interest, but Clamor ain't moving. I look down, checkin' him out, and he's, like, staring into a window of this house where there's some kind of nothin' dog peering out the window. Come on, Clamor, I mean who gives a fuck? But my boy is sitting there with this straight-A student look on his face, and the mutt in the window starts wiggin' out, and they have their little conversation draped in silence, but sayin' a lot, I guess, certainly more than me or my folks were at dinner, and much more than Isabel did when she was yappin' her face off about drama. Now, I need movement to think, kid, so I'm sort of temporarily trapped in the thoughts of Clamor, living in his four-legged groove, and, no offense, but I certainly don't want to be thinking about a poodle, or nothing. Got no time for that.

So my eyes wander, 'cause it's clear Clamor just isn't going anywhere, and I look over to the window to the left, and boy, am I happy I do. There's a fire blazing strong in the fireplace, and first I see the fire, and then I can see the reflection it's making in the window, which is my all-time favorite sight of the day. Like watching laundry go around in a dryer, you can find a pattern of motion, and the bewildering puzzle of the fire just transfixes the shit out of me. Damn—if you know the secret, there's probably the most basic reason, as easy as simple addition that'll tell you why the fire is shaped a certain way. We're not trained to think that way, and I don't think any scientist would bother researching it, but the mathematics of fire will tell you a lot about things, I bet. It's all math, man. Fire is science, not poetry. Stare long enough and you'll hear the truth ringing—you'll hear every speck of fire calling out her name. The shadows of the embers come oblong on the shine of the window, like the strands of her hair, maybe. And best of all is the whirling figure eight of fire that is glowing and sparkling like orange crystal, and like I said before, I know it is there only for me. It's scary, like any privilege, to be a witness to the fire in the stars, to the fire in the fireplace, and to the features of every ripple rotating within the lips of every crest of flame everywhere. I don't deserve any of this, but I refuse to argue the evening back to the sky. All this adds up to truth for me, and visions of the dead jes' sway in my head, kid, teasing my ass. Suicide is the most cowardly act in the whole world, yet somehow I still can't help but admire Leonia's bravery. That's fucked up, kid; someone definitely is going to have to explain that one to me real fast. And Leonia, like this Hitchcock flick I saw the other day—I was real into the movie, parts of it, but I just didn't get the ending. Somewhere in the middle of this brainflow, I realize Clamor has been staring at me like I'm some kind of fuckin' moron, 'cause he's been done looking at that little dog, and he wants to get moving already. He's got other things to check out, I mean, I above anyone understand that. And I laugh, embarrassed, and I reach down and grab his ears for a little squeeze—I wouldn't ever hurt the guy, don't worry about it, man. And we move on. I hope I'm not blushing. What does it mean when your own dog can embarrass the shit out of you? Does that mean you're doing something right or something wrong?

So we keep it going for a while, and Clamor eventually takes a shit, which is my favorite to watch, because he's always a little sheepish, and his ears get crooked, like hooks. Plus, before he dumps, he sniffs crazy semicircles in the dirt, tryin' to find the right spot, tryin' to send the right message. And don't make fun of him, either; wouldn't you be a little self-conscious shittin' in the middle of town, for Christ's sake? And he dumps three big logs, and shakes the remainder out, hips lookin' sleek, and then, like I said, we move on. What's the use hanging around? *You* don't sleep where you shit, do you?

And my worst nightmare comes true because as we're walking on a little bit more, this old lady sitting on her porch calls over to us. I mean, come on! Can't she see we're walking? This old lady is motioning over to us like she's got the most important thing in the world to say, and she can't wait another fuckin' second. I don't care what she has to say, unless she's having some kind of attack, it just *can't* be that important. Not to be mean about the whole thing, but even if she is having an attack, what's that got to do with me and Clamor? Stud, you think dogs have upside down priorities, wait 'til you talk to an old lady for a few seconds; it'll blow your mind. Whoops—nice expression, huh? I'm such a moron. But with this lady? All right, bitch, calm down, we're on our way!

"Is that your dog?" This lady croaks that out first thing, man, first thing, voice all phlegmy and full of the vestiges of lost decades of cigarettes and bridge arguments. What is she, a member of the undercover stolen-dog police task force, or something? No, cunt, I sit around walking strange dogs at night for the hell of it. But here's the thing: I don't answer. I pause, I don't say a fuckin' word for five seconds, man, *five!* We're just starin' at each other, and she's lookin' a little confused, waiting for the reply, and it may come and it may not, and I'm the only one here who knows. So, listen up, I'm in front of her stoop, she called us over, her turf, her terms, but guess who's in charge anyway? I wait, the dog waits, she waits. I stare her right in her eyes, which they say you should never do to animals, but to humans it's fine; it's encouraged, even. I mean, they teach that at every junior salesman's conference, I'm told. So, check it out, this old lady is waiting for me. I get to determine what gets said when, why, and how. In charge, baby. Sometimes it's so easy. People are just lining up. Just ask X-Man from the Sapphire's men's room.

"Yeah. He's mine." Mono-fucking-tone. I don't suffer fools, old or no. And I stare at her through my tired, bloodshot eyes, with the riddles of the world weaving in and out of each smoke ring of my breath that soars up through the chilly night.

"He yours?" And I mean, she's screaming, kid. Croakin' from the gut. You know what glottal fry is? I learned all about that in Speech class. "What's his name?" I close my eyes, 'cause she didn't have to go there. This ain't show and tell; it's life and death. Doesn't anyone get it? Usually my eyes keep 'em away, but now, in the black of night, do I gotta wear a neon sign or something? I've been spending the last I don't know how long explaining this whole mess to you, ma', I just want to figure it out for myself. Just need a clue. But these distractions will never do, I don't want to hear about 'em. It's like they detract from the greater purpose.

"Clamor." God, I love that name.

"What a cute name," this one screeches out. Neighbors'll hear her, I swear.

Clamor's a cute name? Oh, Jesus, I must have missed something, I must have forgot to carry the fuckin' one on that noise, 'cause the word "clamor" couldn't have any less to do with that which is cute. If I'd known that someone, anyone, anywhere on this Earth would have thought for a second that Clamor could possibly be described as cute, I would have tossed in the towel and called him Scruffles, or something like that. Forget about it. "Seafood's good for the blood, young man. Good for you." Now what the fuck is this one here talking about, kid? We're talking about my dog, and she brings that shit up? What the fuck? I think that's called senility in this culture, but if I, age twenty-one, had said some such shit like that, they'd have carted my ass away, man, no thought about it, and I'd have encouraged it. Seafood, man? And she continues, even, "What, is your father or grandfather a clammer?" What is this bitch talking about? "Do you know," she says, "in my day, the gentlemen had clammer pants: they didn't go past the knee, that was the type of pants those kinds of fishermen wore. All the boys had a pair of clammers. Everyone owned clammers." I'm fuckin' trying to walk off the crater in my heart that's been there since the suicide, and I end up in a piss-poor Abbott and Costello skit with the fuckin' poster old lady for Alzheimer's. I don't mean to be mean, but that just ain't what I need at this point, you know where I'm coming from, don't you?

"No, no, ma'am, not a clammer. *Clamor!*" I shout it out. Not to be rude, but, you know.

"Oh, like the magazine? You are a clever young man. That's so cute!"

And I turn around, seething, and just walk away, as she calls after me, laughin', clueless, as tears of poisoned frustration fill my eyes, my teeth rigid and separated. My Timberlands pound away, percussion to my thoughts, my mind is scrambled, off any known beaten track, and uh-oh, now it's gonna be a while before I get set again, don't you think?

And the stars that had shown and shone for me are now cackling in this weird glow-in-the-dark mockery, and the sincere smile of the moon turns to one of derision, and then Clamor, my baby, walks up to a Yield sign and lifts his leg up, way the fuck up there, and lets fly a pale laser, replete with the parabola of piss—again I'm talkin' math—and it glistens in the coming headlights of a rambling U-Haul. I'm fuckin' blinded, 'cause for some reason I look right into the lights, like the secret to the universe was in there, or something, and I start to laugh a bit at myself, rubbing the pain out of my eyes. Clamor looks up, way confused, and I laugh a little more, until he jumps up, wanting to join in whatever fun the poor guy thinks I'm having, getting his muddy claws and heavy paws all the fuck over my wine-red. It's called bonding, in case you were curious, and it sure is welcome. God, that nonchalant look on Clamor's face when he takes a piss gets me every time.

Up the block from my house, there's this huge cemetery, just beyond the dead-end sign. I mean, what kind of real estate geniuses are my parents? They buy a house sixty fuckin' yards from a cemetery? Or was that one of those things that was supposed to build character, you know? Yeah, you got a six-year old? Hell, bring him up with a sense of reality— teach him all about death. Surprised my parents didn't read me Dylan Thomas or Poe as bedtime stories to soothe me, the way they act. People amaze me sometimes. Anyway, me and Clamor end all our walks going through the aisles of the cemetery, checkin' out trees and statues and flowers and whatever is out there. My folks aren't too into me having the dog piss all over the cemetery, out of respect for the dead.

Well, they can think whatever, but I have more respect for the living, and if the dog needs to fuckin' piss, and chooses to do it on some rock with a dead guy's name, well then, my man is going to get rinsed off a little bit, and I got no problem with that. So I don't say nothin' and Clamor stays cool and smirking, and everyone's happy.

I can remember one Halloween when I was a little kid, maybe twelve, and this bigger guy who kind of aspired to be town bully was daring all of us little kids to run through the cemetery alone. He was like sixteen, tellin' all my friends that no one has ever run through there on Halloween and made it back alive, and who is going to be the first to make it? All the kids were saying no, gettin' real scared, one guy was crying, and the bully told us he'd beat the shit out of us all if one of us didn't go there and back to prove our bravery. What kind of logic that was, I don't know, but he picked up my boy Robby, and started shaking the shit out of him. I told the guy to settle down, 'cause I'd do it. What did I give a shit? I had been there at night a million times, and nothing was gonna happen just 'cause it was Halloween, I mean, I might have been young, but I wasn't an idiot or anything. So I take off and come back like ten minutes later with a big smile on my face, and all my friends come over, now everyone crying, hugging me and all shit like that. The bully wanna-be just sits there for some reason, and he looks paralyzed with fear. He must have thought I was a goner. I'm so juiced I turn right around and go for another jog, kid, there and back, and return to a standing fuckin' O. Bully and all. Thinkin' about it, I wonder why bullies never hang around with kids their own age. Probably the same reason that men tend to marry women two, three years younger than them.

And this time, Clamor and I enter the cemetery through

the hole in the fence, and the whole landscape comes wide open in front of us. The darkness is its own language, and the moon is shining over part of the hills and flatlands of New Jersey. At least I think that's New Jersey over there, but you can't tell. You have no sense of direction or distance on a night like this, man, and I've lived in this place just about my whole life. We walk to the top, like we always do, and this time, I let Clamor set the pace. He sniffs a little of everything, and if he's anything like me, he's happy to be here, because he knows there aren't any old ladies or poodles or drama theorists here. Best of all, it's so, so quiet—no one speaking. Just the skyway and a million graves, one for each chamber of my heart that Leonia closed off to the world.

As we make the last few steps, the sky slips, and the mist evolves into a drizzle, and we act like we don't notice. We have to make it to the top. The dead winds just make me tired, and my defenses drop the length of a rainbow, and the thoughts rush back, eager to hammer me into a thin sheet of fool's gold. But I'll wait with Clamor until the sky is drained of its rain, man, I don't give a shit. Let me scope the grave-yard, let me find the perfect place to dig a grave for Leonia. That's funny to even suggest, because she didn't go out like that at all. You know, she went up in smoke, per her majesty's request. I was out of the loop, because her family kind of froze me out of the proceedings. But what, you don't exactly attend a cremation do you, in a suit and all? Some people may, but I certainly don't, I'll tell you that straight off, that's no hobby of mine; it's not supposed to be some big party. Lots of people want to turn everything into a ceremony. So, no grave was good enough for Leonia, if you want to put it like that. Shit, all these graves—one of them must contain Leonia, it seems, but they'll bust you for looking underground, diggin' shit up, and I don't blame 'em, really. Whatever. I spit high in the air, the arc staggers the glow of a street lamp. I can see my spit is green. Don't panic, all it is is the soup. One of these days I gotta ask my ma what the fuck she puts in that pea soup. Then again, what for? Who cares?

I turn around and squint at the green back fence. Believe it or not, there's a backwards swastika and a "Led Zep" written in the same black spray paint. Backwards swastika? I guess it's the thought that counts, eh? Not to be frivolous, but both offend me equally, actually the "Led Zep" one even more. See, the swastika, the guy did just to get a rise. You know deep down he's no Nazi sympathizer; he's just a stupid punk. With the Led Zep one, he really wanted to make a statement. What kind of thought process someone must have to spray paint in a cemetery I'll never know. When are they going to paint that shit over? The graffiti is the gospel of the graveyard, no way you can get around that. It sets the tone. I can't hang around there much longer, you can just about feel the hatred that kid had when he sprayed it. The way he did the "p" at the end of "Zep," it's so clear that he is filled with bad thoughts, at least he was when he wrote it. If you really concentrate on those two instances of graffiti, really concentrate, you'll see that "Led Zep" is totally more a message of hate than the swastika. Look over at that "p," it's all pointed and jagged, with thin streams of black spray paint coming off the bottom. Bad vibes just emanatin' off that thing like crazy, it just knocks me out. One of these days, I bet Robert Plant'll be walking these paths, checking up on a dead relative, maybe, and see his band's name written there, and then the swastika, and then just wonder why the fuck he got into the music business in the motherfucking first place.

And wouldn't you know it, things just get worse. I walk by this enormous statue of Jesus Christ, with his arms outstretched overlooking his flock, protecting the masses, in bronze, and guess what? Some joker must have took a bat or an ax or something to it, and knocked off his head, and then stole it. I'm trying to make a connection, see what message this adds up to. It ain't easy to make a prayer upon the statue of a decapitated Christ, and I'll tell you, I'm not even gonna try right now. This is just the kind of thing that the Daily News would flip over: *Headless Christ in Graveyard Heist!* Well, I sit down with Clamor, and the rain picks up another little bit. I don't blame it. I'm staring up at the Jesus, who still has those arms outstretched as if nothing happened, still doing his job, in a way. And me, I can't treat the Leonia stuff all so seriously now, because I'm worrying about the head, and I can feel the anger traveling into my gut, and then up to my head, and then I clench down on Clamor's leash—it's the law in New Jersey, kid, you gotta have it on, no matter where you are or what time it is—and I think of the kid that sprayed the shit, and I think of the prick who took the head, and you don't have to be Encyclopedia Brown to know it was the same punk on the same night, the same six-pack of Michelob that did it for him (like $5.99, probably at Garden State Farms down the block), that convinced him it was the right thing to do. I hate America. America sucks, man. Who the fuck dreams up schemes like stealing Jesus' head, I just cannot begin to imagine. And I realize Clamor is looking up at me, wondering what I'm so pissed about, because I don't think the statue ever meant that much to him, at least not as far as I can see. But fuck it, what am I, gonna let it bother me if some guy sucks down some beers and sprays on the wall and then decapitates Jesus? He wins if I get all crazy about it. Plus, what's that cat doin' to me, personally? Shit, all I can do is hope the head brings the crook some luck, hope he displays it and can tell the story in an entertaining way, and all. With "Stairway to Heaven" playing in the background—yeah, I can picture it. But with all the meetings my mom attends around town, wouldn't you at least think they could get someone to build a new head for the thing?

And I say, "Let's go, Clammer," old lady style, just to see if he notices, but he doesn't. He just leads the way. I'm so proud of him, walking through the cemetery at night, his coat accepting the thin, diagonal rain without dispute. I love my faithful dog. And come to think of it, tonight, the silence wasn't the best thing for me. Maybe I should have chosen the golf course, not the cemetery. More people, more traffic. Fewer dead bodies. I know bad decisions can fuck you up big time, but I can't dwell on that right now. If I put myself down too much, I may never be able to get back up. Well, this is a cemetery, it ain't a playground. Ah, cemetery, playground, what's the difference? One makes you feel young, and the other lifts your spirits, I guess. No need, man, for this lame-ass cemetery-pondering, with the caves from my dreams revisiting me once again. And the temperature must have dropped in a big way, 'cause I'm all chattery, and I can tell Clamor picks up the pace. Jesus, it's fuckin' cold out here, man! I look up at the sky: our moon sweetly folds, and here comes the winter.

What a lopsided romance Leonia and I had. The way I figure, in order to abuse someone, the first step, way before the actual abuse, is to convince them that they deserve it.

And afterwards, convince them that it wasn't abuse. And you know what? It is so easy to convince someone to believe something they want to believe in the first place. That's another thing they must go over at salesman conventions. But in order to make someone laugh, you have to get them to like you. In order to beat the shit out of someone, you have to get them to love you. All these hippie songwriters sayin' there's a thin line between love and hate just don't get it. Man, they must be living in the middle ages, as far as I'm concerned. I don't even know why the English language has two separate words for those concepts. They're one and the same, only claim to fame is who do you blame?

And we go home, and Mom is reading the newspaper, every article, every word, every ad. She knows the world better than anyone, but she knows thanks to second-hand accounts. Safer that way; I don't blame her. My only gripe is that people who sleep under the blanket of conformity may rest easy, get their eight hours, but their dreams are dull, I mean, we all know that, right? Mom looks up at me, happy we're back, and gets up to get me a towel. Dad's downstairs watching the game, or something. In hiding, so to speak. I say my hellos and Clamor collapses on the rug for the night. I go over to the bookcase, steal a couple Mississippi John Hurt albums, and think I'll be alone, maybe collapse for the night myself. Yeah, the kid'll just be upstairs, listening to some fingerpickin' folk-blues. Who's going to complain about that?

So, music on low, I'm up in bed, flipping through *Songs of Innocence* and *Songs of Experience*. William Blake, my man—I can read, you know—and these poems are just always there for me. I don't consider myself a big poetry guy, even, but Blake, man, he's been a big help. If he didn't die a few hundred years ago, he'd definitely get fan mail from me, I can tell you that. But all that doesn't add up to too much right now, because Izzy comes right in, a little afraid. I'm almost happy she didn't knock. First of all, it would have spoiled my image of her—she's a non-knocker, that's all there is to it. Number two, to be honest with all parties involved, if anyone knocked, I likely would have pretended I was asleep, just to avoid the conversation. Who needs dialogue? My girlfriend's dead, if you haven't heard, buddy. And Izzy comes in, with her short hair shaped like a helmet, the back of it shaved a little bit—is that the style these days?—and she looks at me and points, her long index finger blazing in at me. She smiles. Uh-oh, right, that's what I'm thinking. And she leans over and says, "I got something for you tomorrow—you're gonna be here tomorrow, right?" I shrug. Hey, pretty cool. Does she get my point? Do you? How the hell do I know anymore if anyone's gonna be anywhere tomorrow? Isabel is not fazed, never mind my attempted philosophy. "Tomorrow," she repeats, firmer, almost as a threat. And she is gone.

By the time my ma gets to bed, I would guess Pop's in his second or third r.e.m. cycle, so they're in the same geographic location, on the same piece of furniture, but let's be honest about this: is it really like the way they used to go to bed when they were nervous, when they were first dating? I'm sure it was a lot more fun then. Leonia and I, man, we used to have a lot of fun, especially when we went to bed. I mean, sometimes we would go to bed on a Friday, and not think to get out of bed until a few days later, if that's what we were into. That all changed, I can tell you that. The way it ended was pretty sad: I used to make love, and she would just make believe, and then we would talk about it together, and just make excuses. It really changed, I can tell you. The thing is, it all happens so gradually, it's all so sneaky, that there's no way to keep a beat on it. A lot of big, big mistakes went unchecked, if you want to put it that way.

And it's been a while since there's been any movement downstairs, so I go to the bathroom, without the Blake. I mean, Ma usually keeps a crossword down there or something. I should be able to pass the time. And there's really no question about it, I simply don't, do not, feel well at all. Was it the bouncer or still the Daniels, I don't know, but I feel like I been through something. And I sit on the bowl, and the bowl is *low,* practically resting on the tile floor, you know what I mean? It feels like I'm in some fuckin' nursery school or something. Well, I guess that makes a lot of sense, I mean, I did use it when I was four years old, when I took my first shit in an actual toilet, and my dad congratulated me by walking me down to the candy store to buy a pack of base-ball cards—where *are* those fuckin' things these days any-way, they must be worth a fortune. So I let go, and I guess the split-pea is over and out, and as I'm on the toilet, I think of Clamor earlier in the night, how he was so much cooler than I was doin' this activity, how he made a cute face, and moved on. Me, it's hurting as it comes out, stings and scratches, and I can feel my whole body working, which it really shouldn't. It should be a relief, but it's an effort, and I can feel sweat sizzling on my forehead, and I can feel my hands tense up like mofoes as they grip the side of the toilet, and my eyes are closed, in silent fear, and I can hear every nerve and gastral juice working inside my stomach, trying to make some sense of signals that they are not used to getting. Is this my third shit since Leonia happened? Fourth, maybe? Can't say, dude, can't say for sure. I don't keep track.

And I feel like I'm getting a headache and a fever, and I hope that the 'rents and Isabel don't realize that I'm taking a while in here. Thing about this house is it's a little like the universe—you do one thing to one part of it, and whether you know it or not, it makes some sort of impact on every little corner of the cosmos, no matter how far away. Man, this house is the home of the creaks, and I know as the soup and various innards are being expelled, my family probably winces as they can hear the churns of my stomach echo through all the walls in all the caverns in the place. And I know there's lots more to go, I know I could be there forever and never be done with this shit, but sometimes you just gotta draw the line, is all. And I wipe, and glance at the paper to see if it's green or something, but it's not: it's dark fuckin' red, with solid pieces of blood and all sorts of other stuff in there. My heart drops with fear and here comes more sweat, plus tears to the surface. I close my eyes and throw my head back, letting gravity guide the bloody toilet paper between my thighs into the pink water. Oh, man, that is really disappointing. Blood? I thought all that was over, son, I really did.

So when I'm done with it all, I get up and stare in the mirror. This reminds me of the way I was on the bus, and I wonder why I bothered coming home in the first place. Was I looking for some kind of answer that I thought somehow my folks could help me with? Come on, man, these people didn't even bring up Leonia's name, for fuck's sake. Now, in all fairness, man, neither did I—leave it to me to look for sympathy out of this whole deal. Man, that's the sign of a really shitty person, so strike that shit. Anyway, I'm staring in the mirror, and all the defiance is gone. I'm trying to be perfectly still, but my shoulders slump, and the reflection is weakening, makin' faces back at me, faces of contempt, faces of disgust. I'm in the same bathroom I used twenty years ago, and I don't feel any older, any wiser, any surer of who I am. Way less, if you want to know the truth. I never had these thoughts when I was a kid. I keep looking in the mirror, but I'm really torturing myself with it, because it makes me more depressed and more depressed and more depressed. And as I keep the stare going, my eyes dissolve, and then my face dissolves, and then the mirror dissolves, and then the wall dissolves, and I can see so clearly the 'rents, Mom and Dad, in their bed, sleeping side by side, ass to ass, snoring to their respective walls, probably dreaming about ex-significant others, and all their old crushes. And now you see exhibits A and B about love and hate being one and the same. You think Leonia hated me? Of course she did, she killed herself over me. You think Leonia loved me? Of course she did, motherfucker, she killed herself over me, didn't she?

And I keep staring into the mirror, thinking of the rotten blood misplaced in my body, not behaving, not remaining in the veins, as it is trained to, but instead all over the fuckin' place, man, all fuckin' up my system. I can tell you, it's doin' all kinds of crazy shit in there, man. I can taste the salt of blood at the base of my throat, can feel the thickness on the back of my tongue. And now, ever since the flush, my blood is flowing through the pipes and through the New Jersey sewage system, and will probably end up in the Atlantic Ocean, if I'm lucky. I can't swim, by the way, never learned. And I'm not trying to freak you out or anything, but the quieter it gets in this place, the clearer I can hear the voice of the headless Christ telling me he loves me, and I can hear the voice of the devil—standin' there with Jesus' head under his arm—telling me softly that I should cut off the arms of the statue, too, and telling me that I should write some shit of my own on the cemetery wall, and that there's nothing wrong with it because the God I know and the God I think of as God let Leonia's stray thoughts become Leonia's deeds and let her deeds become her legacy and then let all that shit become my own barbed-wire fate. God's voice. Devil's voice. Man, they both sound the same: too good to be true. Shit, tonight, I try to convince myself I feel one up on the devil, like there's no way he's gonna touch me. No way. I ain't sure if God's on my side, but I just want everybody within shouting distance to know, for real, that I am on His side, I want that perfectly clear. Kid, I ain't defecting just 'cause things didn't work out for me this time, in this case. But now I'm in a grudge match, a rematch of the stare down with myself. Looking through my eyes, which isn't hard to do at this point, and I look straight through to the midnight of my mind, the shadow of each crease of my brain. And the room gets darker, as God and the devil struggle for my affection, and I struggle just to remain. I live in sanity's doghouse and I must win the stare down with myself.

I reach under the bathroom drawer, where I kept it in store from before, and take Leonia's gun out, take the fun out, but who's gonna clean up my broken brains when they all run out? I'm gonna win this one big; you watch. Wasn't I in this situation just a while ago? And, yeah, I'm twitching hard as I look up and I feel the cold steel in my right hand, and boy, does it feel good. Sure, I'm twitching, all right, I ain't gonna play like I'm the cool one around here. And I point the gun at the mirror and it's great, 'cause I can see the hammer and the barrel, depending on where I look. It's the best of both worlds, man, I can get it coming and going like you wouldn't believe. I keep my trembling hand as steady as possible, and move my head around subtly, so this triple vision doesn't get disturbed. Now, here's something I can grab onto, man, I can see every sliver of silver, and it looks so good. It looks sweet, I mean, look at it! Who do you think designed these things? Why would they design them like that? Jesus, man, this is pretty wild. I'm doing different poses, man, and I could be all the heroes of our lives: Rambo, Bond, anyone, man. A gun is the means to a fantasy. It opens up worlds as it closes others. But why would someone think to carry a gun if they weren't planning on using it; I mean what would be the purpose? What would be the aim? And I really think I'm winning the stare down, kid, I think I've got him on the ropes, I think I've got him singin' SOS to his echo, man. Oh, what's that you're thinking; I'm cheating 'cause I have a gun? Yeah, you're right, but we know my reflection would have kicked my ass again big time if I didn't have one. I don't consider it cheating at all, because all's fair in love and hate.

When was the last time I took a breath? Man if you're going to take a last breath, make sure every trace of oxygen in the room enters your lungs. You gotta take that last breath like you mean it. I really don't want my last breath to be in this room, full of the memories and stink of the split-pea shit and the blood in the paper that should have stayed in my body. So I get a better grip on the gun, and whirl the motherfucker around and stick it right in my mouth, doing my best Leonia imitation, like it's the biggest, coldest, most metallic lollipop in life's long history. .38s, man, they got a flavor about them. I'm pressing the barrel against the roof of my mouth until it hurts just 'cause of all the pressure. See the sinews and shit in my forearm ripplin'? Now, for the first time in a while, I like the way I look. I might walk around with a gun hanging out of my mouth all the time, everywhere—it's a good addition. Leonia, if she were here, would call it *accessorizing*. And I steal a steely glance over at the mirror; who's gonna blink now, big guy? And my finger tenses on the trigger, and I finger the beautiful smooth curve of the trigger, each point, each undulation. I'm moving the trigger almost enough but not quite—how much pressure do you need for this thing to go off, man, I don't even know? What's a torque? We're not back to math again, are we? There's just no escape, son. And my finger is tappin' the trigger, just testing it, and the hammer is winking on top of the gun, and the barrel and its son, the bullet, knows just the spot in the top of my head that it's gonna blast through, and just the impressionist image on the wall that it's gonna paint with the colors of my tainted brain. So, just as a surprise, I look right into the eyes in the mirror, and my reflection is trembling until it's blurry. And do you wanna hear the best part of all? That sloppy son of a bitch puts his hands over his eyes, turning away, like he doesn't want to see it all happen. He doesn't have the balls to be there up close when all the shit comes crashing down. I take the gun out from deep between my lips, and I can feel the reverberations of my heart beating wildly in the roof of my mouth, up there where the gun was, and through my workshirt, and all over the walls of this little bathroom. I smile big again, like I *been* through something. I put the gun back under the drawer. You know what all this means, don't you? It means I win. Again. It means I ain't goin' out like that, bitch. I wouldn't even give you the satisfaction.

THE GRIDS OF THE SKY

I've got this great picture—black and white—above my bed in New Jersey of a young Pete Townshend, arms in the air, caught right in the middle of destroying his guitar. It's amazing, because there's utter chaos on stage, I mean, smoke and debris everywhere, and it's like only Pete is calm. Now, that's an expensive guitar, and he just goes ahead and wrecks it? I've always wondered why he used to do that. I used to think it was just a random act of violence, taking out frustration (originally real, later manufactured) on something that couldn't fight back. It could fuckin' explode on him, maybe, but it couldn't fight back. And then my peripheral vision—what a stupid invention, man, if I wanted to see something I'd have looked there in the first place—picks up Leonia's high school graduation picture tacked up on the other end of the wall. And my eyes dart back and forth between the two pictures, the look of concentration on Pete's face, the slightly fatigued smile on Leonia's—man, that bastard of a photographer should have taken it a second sooner, it would have been better that way, would have been *real*. Pete amid the amazing destruction is somehow triumphant. And at the same time, Leonia, sweater-clad, made-up, wearing a long skirt that flows, I bet, like she always did, is so clearly aglow in sadness, like sitting for a class picture is just another disadvantage to living. But why is her quiet gloom amidst a placid scene so similar to Pete's stoic face amidst a war zone? I'm so confused, but I know there's a link between the two pictures, I know there's some sort of reason I put 'em near each other, on the same wall. My pop always says that everything happens for a reason, and it's true; I've come to agree with him at least on that—the reasons are right there; it all depends on your effort, how much you want to hustle trying to figure it all out.

And for this one, the Townshend/Leonia thing, I'm trying my hardest, honest to God. I close my eyes and lay back on my bed, wondering what I ever saw in the Townshend picture in the first place. The Who were an okay band to me, I mean, "Squeeze Box" and all, but why put the picture up? It's that concentration, I think. I must have related at the time, or, I don't know, maybe I just thought it was cool to break things. But I close my eyes and try to imagine playing a two-hour concert of some of the greatest rock-n-roll music mankind has ever heard, I'm talkin' true art, and then demolishing the instrument that brought so much magic into the room. What ever would cause someone to do that? It would seem to me you'd want to just hang on to the guitar, baby it, make sure no harm whatsoever comes to it. But why be upset at it? Why the anger? Wait, hang on, I think I got it! Do you know why he destroyed his guitar, I bet? It's maybe 'cause he expressed himself as best he could, wrote all the songs he needed to write, left his very soul on stage for cheering fans to see, and guess what? After all that, it just wasn't *enough*. And I open my eyes and they flicker to pretty Leonia.

And Hurricane Isabel storms right into the room, opens the door, no problem with her conscience at all, you see, and the dog follows, all jingling and panting, and I guess the day has begun by default for me, because I certainly didn't think I wanted it to, just yet. I mean, not to whine, but I've been through some pretty heavy shit that needs to get worked out. And Isabel kneels down at the side of my bed and leans forward, as if to tell me a secret. What, is the dog gonna hear or something? But that's the thing—dogs fuckin' *get it* when they're not supposed to know something, and it's Psychology fuckin' 101, acted out for all to see right here in my bedroom, man. Clamor gets super psyched, and goes bat-shit and tries to horn in on the action, managing to lick both our faces with one gigantic swipe of the tongue. I push the guy away—with love, you understand—and look at my sister. What the fuck is so important? Silence establishes control, or at least gives the appearance of it, which in practice is as good as the real thing. Think about it, who are the people who really scare you; are they the talkers, the yellers, the threateners, or are they the listeners, the thinkers, and the glarers? Rhetorical, man, don't sweat the answer.

"OK, today I'm taking you on a walk—trust me, I know what you need." Hear that? Little sister knows what I need. Leonia, dead and gone forever, but all I need is to stretch my legs a little, yeah, that makes sense; that'll do. A walk. Like Clamor. Whatever. Leonia scattered and my life shattered, and Isabel cruisin' the house as if she was the only thing that mattered. Figures, totally figures. Well, with a walk, it won't get Leonia off my mind, but it will get Isabel off my back, and I'll settle for that much. Isabel, man. Thing is, I know I wasn't half as cocky as that when I was her age. If I had an older brother or sister, I imagine I would have, like, deferred, especially in times like this, I mean, no offense, but what does the kid know?

There's really no arguing with her. I slip away, go down the stairs and head straight for the bathroom—no hellos just yet—and turn the water on for a shower. I strip without breaking stride, like a transparent snake molting, or something like that; you know what I mean, and I sneak a glance at the mirror on the way to the shower. Shit, I'm a skinny motherfucker; but I feel good. I wonder how it must feel to be substantial. Maybe, hopefully, one of these days we'll even find out. I wink in the mirror. Ha! My reflection knows I kicked the motherloving shit out of it last night—I can shower here without shame. I turn the water on and there's that little jet of water that immediately shoots out and hits the back of the hand that turned the faucet on. Feels good, but so, so foreign, as if a chocolate milkshake is shooting out of that nozzle. Imagine me forgetting what taking a damn shower feels like, unbelievable, man. And I get in the tub all at once, one motion, no wincing, just like I used to jump into the Atlantic Ocean down the shore on vacation. I used to see some people there methodically bathe themselves in the water so their body temperatures would adjust slowly. You could see 'em dip their hands into the sea and then rub the moisture on their bodies, making faces and shit—fuck that! I'm *in!* I don't wait for nothing! And as I'm in the shower, I imagine washing not dirt off me, but days. I'm washing events off me, not sweat. I use Isabel's shampoo—goddamn, look at the price on this shit, fuckin' ridiculous, it all ends up in the Atlantic anyway—and it smells all fruity, like something citrus, and I can't imagine that scientists would work so hard to invent such a smell. I mean, is it just me, or aren't there still a couple of diseases out there they can work on?

It's a powerful smell, but in kind of a good way, though, and I mean I'm really grinding it into every cell of my scalp, and each fraction of each strand of my hair, and I work it in big time. I'm determined to smell great, and it's going to be the first time in a while. I give it a big rinse, and the spray of water makes the soreness on my head sting (motherfucker of a bouncer; did you get his name, man?), and when the shampoo slides down my body—front, back, sides—the invisible caked vomit and come and tears and blood and saliva and urine and God knows what else slowly erode, but I'm sure only partially. I don't scrub, and I don't lather too much, don't even *want* to totally wash the last few days off. I don't want to wash Leonia away, let her slide down the drain. Shit, now that I think of it, what was so wrong with my head smelling like a fire hose in the first place, man? Should I even have taken a shower? But I turn around and let a lot of water run down my back and into the crack of my ass, pulling the sucker apart as far as it'll go. But let's be honest, how do I really know if the water is reaching the dried blood there? I mean, there's just no way to tell.

I step out of the shower, and I look at myself in the mirror, and there's no fogging there whatsoever because I don't take really hot ones, and I look at myself, and man, damned if I don't look kind of good. My hair is fucked up just right, and I look clean, ready to attack the day. What Isabel has in mind, I have no idea, but I'm sure it has something to do with drama, or her new friends or something like that. Who's to say? Who's gonna argue? I don't care, man, it's a nice enough day, I'm up for anything. Well, except maybe drama.

An old black T-shirt was lying around in my old dresser, and it fits baggy, just the way I like it. Same jeans I been wearing all along, which don't feel so good, to be honest, but I do a couple of deep knee bends, and things click. Steal some of Pops' white socks (I don't trust any other kind) and his old paper boy hat—backwards, man, *always* backwards—and I'm down the stairs. Mom smiles at me 'cause of the hat and points to the bagels on the table, but I just don't have the time, man; I'm on the run. I know some mothers take it personally if you don't eat—and I know and appreciate that my ma made the effort—but I'm just not sure I'm that hungry, and I mean, I hate to bring this up, but what happens if I have a couple bagels, then a few hours later, what then? The blood, right?

When I get outside, Isabel is sitting under a tree like a three-year old, legs sticking straight out, feet pointing to the sky. I don't know, it sure doesn't look comfortable to me, but maybe they do some kind of flexibility training in her drama department, how am I supposed to know? And she's breathing deeply with her eyes closed, with this otherworldly grin on her face. If we got an agenda, we got one, and let's get to it. I ain't gonna spend my day watching some chick breathe, even if it is my sister. But for some reason, just before I was gonna march right on over there and de-trance her, I do, in fact, just sit there and watch her. She's so peaceful, like she somehow got rid of all the bones in her body—it's all just saggin' so free right now. Maybe I should join drama, because I certainly am never that calm. Being relaxed like that is a good thing, for sure, or at least the ability to become that relaxed is definitely a plus.

And my mind kind of jumps to the word "suicide," and for some reason I do like a Boolean word search of all the times I used the word in my life in conjunction with all the times I used it while talking to Leonia. I think I can remember one, no, *two*. Once, I told her she was the type of person that would proofread a suicide note. Man, that was mean, no two ways about it. I can be a bastard on occasion, especially 'cause not only do I put someone down, but I mean sometimes I really do go the extra mile, and do it in a creative, actually thoughtful way. Pointless. The other time we talked about suicide might have been our second or third date, and I was telling her about my cousin on my dad's side and my aunt on my mom's side, both of whom killed themselves. Those were sad stories, even though I didn't know the cousin in Italy and wasn't too close to the aunt. Didn't go to either funeral, by the way.

I look at Isabel, studying her, hoping suicide isn't a hereditary trait. Does suicide, like baldness, skip generations? It's gonna skip me, man, I can promise you that right now, but if there's one thing I learned, I'm not going to speak for anyone else—they'll have to tell you for themselves. Oh, man, do me a favor—if you ever see her, ask Isabel if she'll make you the same promise I just did. Seriously. I've always thought that whenever there's a killing, that somehow the assassin must resemble the victim, and never is that more true than with suicide. I don't remember if I read that in some book or I thought of that on my own. Hey, to be honest with you, I'm not even in the mood to talk about suicide, so I'd rather just put that off for another time.

So I go over to Izzy and shake her a little and she opens her eyes, gets a pissy look and motions me to sit down by slapping the lawn. I sit where she slaps. She goes into her backpack and busts out like this plastic bag within a plastic bag within a plastic bag, so the contents are kind of blurry, but it looks like sticks and plants and dirt, things like that. Isabel looks up with a grin, but like a Hollywood grin, not a brother-sister grin. Pseudo-smiles have the opposite effect on me, and I really don't like to see my sister wearin' them. Shit like that worries me. Let's keep an eye out.

"Mushrooms. I got 'em from a friend. You ever take 'em at school?" Isabel is not just askin' to ask; she's askin' to know, wants me to say no, and then to say yes to the mushrooms. It's my nature to flush the bastards down the toilet so she can't do 'em, but really, when you stop to think about the whole thing, who cares? What's that gonna help matters? I've done worse myself, and if she likes it, let her do it, why hassle her about it? Sex, drugs, creative writing, diet—everything else, too, maybe—these are things that if you like it you should do it, and if you don't like it, you shouldn't, that's all. But to talk someone out of it, or to make someone feel guilty about it? That's fucked. And honestly? I've never eaten mushrooms, but I've heard about 'em, even had the chance to do them once or twice. An old friend of mine took his SATs on shrooms and aced the math but fucked up on the verbal. He used one of my number two pencils, also, which should probably count for something. Now that I mention it, you think that guy really was on shrooms? I mean, I didn't see him eat them, and I'm normally the type of person who needs to see things for myself. Anyway, don't get me wrong, 'cause I'm not trying to say I've never taken drugs; I have, all through school I have, from time to time, no big deal. Mushrooms, man, it's not like I wouldn't—it's just like I didn't. And my reflexes, the instincts of my bones and joints, tell me just to tell Izzy no. I know she means well, but I don't think a week after someone dies you should go ahead and trip, I just don't think that's how it's supposed to go. So how'm I gonna put this to her?

"You wanna do mushrooms? I don't know, man; I think

that might be an insult to the dead." In fairness, Leonia did die, but on purpose—an insult to the living. Weak argument on my part. My Logic professor would have called that a "straw man." It's like I'm begging to be talked into it. She knows it, too.

"An *insult?*" Stage whisper. Don't know what, but something I said struck some kind of chord in Isabel. Or maybe it was just those breathing exercises. "I'd be honored if I could confuse someone enough to cause them to delve into themselves to try to solve my essence by taking mushrooms."

What? I think a lot of girls think shit like that, but who but an outlaw plays mind games for fun? Who lives to mind-fuck other people, I just don't know, man, I just think that's sad. My baby sister is slipping, man. And I look up at the front door about twenty yards away, and I see my mom, blurry, beaming through the screen door, watching her two kids talking under the tree, the way we used to do it fifteen years ago, probably. But we weren't talking about mushrooms and dead people then. You gotta understand; Isabel wasn't an actress back then. So I look away from Ma, and then I can imagine Leonia the Omnipresent watching this scene in her box seat, watching everything and passing judgment like crazy and maybe getting one last chuckle (who says it'll be the last, come to think of it) that she can control me from the dead better than she could ever control me face-to-face. Hey, that may be The Reason right there, but no, I can't accept that. If she wanted to say "fuck you," then why didn't she just come out and say it? Funny thing is, the shit Isabel was saying, what, would she say it's some sort of compliment if someone kills herself over you? Should I be flattered? Come on, what kind of reality is that? So my face swivels into a snarl, and the resentment of Leonia's dirty

trick turns into a dominating caring for my sister, a fascina-
tion of drugs' benefits, and a general love of the unknown
within the known. I reach for the plastic bag. My face is still,
and I'm serious about this. I can feel (peripheral vision
again—but this time it's good) Izzy trained in on me, and
both of us know if there's any kind of trip, I have to be the
captain of it; that's just the way it is, the way it's always been.

"No!" Stage whisper again; someone's gotta talk to her
about that, it's no good. "We have to do it with this." And
wouldn't you know it, she pulls out a Snickers, holds it up
with a lot of flair, and rips the wrapper off. A Snickers bar!
Isn't Isabel great? Thing about mushrooms, who cares if our
'rents are watching? They wouldn't know what the hell we
were doing. It ain't like we're injecting the shit. No needles
at all, kid. You could be walkin' by, and all you'd think is
that we're eating a damn chocolate bar. And the shrooms? I
mean, a mushroom's a mushroom, portobello or whatever, I
bet you wouldn't know the difference yourself. She's being
real careful, like a surgeon, trying to divide the Snickers
evenly. Concentrating like Townshend, gotta say. I don't
even like chocolate, but a ritual is a ritual, it might be stupid,
but it's habitual, so don't even think, you just gotta go ahead
with it—that's the American way, right? Which reminds
me, if I ever have kids, there is no way I'm going to make
any school force them to say the pledge of allegiance. They
tricked my dad into becoming an American citizen—something about tax inheritance law, some bullshit like that. They
made him say the pledge, stripped him of his heritage. I'm
totally against that. Mandated loyalty and patriotism? That's
all wrong. But I'll do Snickers for Isabel—no harm there.

So Isabel puts the shit on top of the bag, I see the um-
brella heads and the stalks, and I take a big bite of my

Snickers and then gobble some of the real shit up. Treat it like it's popcorn, kid, don't worry about it. And I slam the shit down, and Isabel takes about forty, maybe thirty-five percent of it, and I'm on the rest hard. I down the rest of my Snickers, whistle for Clamor, and the three of us are on our way. The prodigal son, the prodigal daughter, and the German Shepherd. You gotta understand—my dog doesn't like people leaving the house unless he comes with. All the people who stop by my house always whine about him being overprotective or nervous or too affectionate, but that always pisses me off. He's a German *Shepherd*. You know what that means? Don't you know what shepherds used to do? You think dogs just forget that shit overnight, man? You can't make an old dog forget old tricks; isn't that obvious?

And we're down the block, but the shrooms of course don't do anything right away, and that's cool for now—cocaine and shit, that'll let you know it's in your system right off the bat. Shrooms kind of hang out before they notify. Isabel was talking about heading over to Wood Park. Don't start freaking out about the name, like the city planners would think of such a stupid name, like, "there's a few trees, so let's just call the shit 'wood.' " Nah, it didn't go down like that at all. The way it actually happened is that there was this rich guy named Wood, and he said he'd give the city planners a mil' or something if they'd put his name on the park. Wait—come to think of it, that's an even stupider reason than if they called it "wood" 'cause of the trees, man. That really bums me out. All when I was a kid, you mean I was really playing in some rich guy's playground? The whole world seems like a playground of the rich. But tell me this—what kind of villain would want his own name on a park, especially if his name is something like "Wood"? I just don't understand it, man; it's totally beyond me. But let's keep in mind that the same city planners who negotiated that brainchild of a deal made sure that a cemetery was built on a dead-end street. Get it? Gallows humor at city hall—tax dollars hard at work, I'm sure. But the three of us are walking quick, and I think Clamor knows we're going to the park—it's not a bad walk—and he likes it there, lots of members of the opposite sex and the same species—two top priorities for my dawg.

For some reason, though, Isabel is I think trying hard to get into the shrooms already. Hope she's not forcing, but she is doin' little deadhead dances, staring at flowers, trees, whatever, doing things that I guess people are supposed to do when they trip. But we're not tripping, at least not yet. I guess she's preparing, like an airplane passenger who keeps the seat belt fastened during a two-hour delay on the runway, just to get in the mood. Anyway, never mind all that; who am I to tell someone how to trip—any way she wants to do it is fine with me, I guess. And like I said, I'm okay right now. There's no effect yet, but I am sweating a little bit, although not the sweat that you normally get when you're your normal self, it's more like a message that the machine of my anatomy is getting revved up for me. The perspiration is a little like crystal, little ice chips, and I can feel it smoldering on my forehead, and gleaming, and I can picture each bead of sweat absorbing strobes of sunshine and reflecting and mirroring them, and the patterns of the atmosphere displayed within the drops in links and chains and prismatic connections, and my forehead feels cool. Not only that, with the sweat, but my armpits are tingling, deep inside, and I can feel energy surrounding my body, like my body is nothing more than rapidly moving particles clumped together temporarily, for the eighty years I'm rumored to be allotted on this planet. Eighty years, of course, unless I fuckin' decide to jump ship, right? Which I won't. And I'm rolling with everything, and I turn to my left to look at Clamor, who stops, makes a perfect arch of a stance with his rear legs, flips his ears back a little, shifts his eyes around to make sure no one (except maybe me) is looking, and then lets go. No blood for Clamor, I notice, lucky dog. Isabel, my younger sister, misses the whole thing.

In my hometown, the powers that be stuck the park right next to the fire station, the recreation center, the library, the liquor store and the police station. That's kind of funny. If you wanted to, you could check out *A Farewell to Arms,* get drunk, bail a hypothetical whore out of jail, and play a pickup game of hoops all within walking distance. I hate the suburbs, but remember what I said about hating something, man, it's like a double-edged kiss. And we walk through the park, and it's not crowded at all, just us, just infant sunshine learning where to glow. We sit down in the grass, and Clamor lays down in front of us, tongue *out,* kid. I look off into the distance. My stomach whirs and dips, and there's an empty, nervous feeling, like taking off in a plane, like being sober and kissing a girl you just met. And so the stomach sinks into the ass, and you gotta understand, man, I'm fuckin' gone. Zoom. Mushrooms, man. I think I ate a lot of that stuff. I look at Isabel and laugh and she looks at me, delighted. She's really excited, happy to get me into a state where we can be together, alone. "Are you there yet?" Isabel asks the question and I just smile wide and stay silent. Let her guess. "Nawww," she says. She doesn't believe it, maybe, but it's true. I grin, still silent. So she sees me smile and finally gets it, finally knows. "Yeah?" *Yeah!*

That spirally feeling I had in my stomach must have been contagious, 'cause I'm now getting it in my legs and my hands and my head. I totally now know the exact meaning of the term "taking drugs." All this time I thought you don't take drugs; drugs take you, but this is sweet, almost summonable. It's better than peripheral vision, man, or blood, which is there when you don't want it to be. Mushrooms are like lots of money in the bank that you can just take from any time you want. And I'm takin'. If you've never shroomed, you may be expecting me to jump off buildings or feel bugs crawlin' on my body, claw my own eyes out, or something, but that's all nightly news garbage—it's really not that big of a deal, you got to trust me. Isabel is doing more breathing exercises, for some reason, stretching her back and stuff. One of her friends from school, I guess, calls to her and Izzy screams out "we're tripping!" which bums me out a lot. You hate to say that another human being is capable of disappointing you, especially family, but she's been doing that a lot lately. Isabel springs up and zigzags her way over to her friend, like halfway across the park. I'm a little weird about that because she and I were gonna have a day, trip together, talk about shit (mention Leonia? she *is* on my mind, you know) and I just know there's no way she can talk to those people for less than forever—that's just the way they are, those people. So to me this is just a huge disappointment, and I am getting these intense down feelings, and I picture myself as the blind conductor on this monstrous Amtrak train speeding on a downhill track, like that's my psyche. Then, I withdraw a little dough, go deep into the mushrooms, the humongous secret of the fungus, and mystically and immediately the train levels, and then rises, and I am alone and flying, and the world is a merry-go-round, a carousel spinning around the sun, and the brass ring is coming into view, gleaming and beckoning; all I got to do is grab it.

In the distance, as I'm looking at Isabel and that other drama chick, I can clearly see five trees lined up right next to each other. This is the craziest thing I've ever seen because the trees are completely different, and it looks like they came out of nowhere. I'm sure I've seen them, climbed them, carved my initials in them before, but I've never actually *seen* them. Now, I don't know that much about trees, but I can see that these are five totally different species. And the thing is, they're right next to each other. Wow, someone must have planted those things on purpose, as a gag or a code or something, I mean, those kinds of trees don't just pop up next to each other like that. Trees have ghettoes just like people; they tend to congregate with the same types, that's just the way they are. So what comes in fives? Fingers, toes, yeah, those trees are the digits on the hand of the park. Where's the limb? The slide? I don't know, man, even the stupid stuff makes sense. I wish Isabel was here, so I could mention it to her. But I gotta tell someone. Five? Five *senses!*

"Clamor, boy, check that out—that tree on the left is sight—look at it, it's flickering like it's my personal star and shining, it's winking at me as I'm looking at it. The eyes in the trees, man, and the one next to it is smell, it radiates this country autumn smell, the aroma of Eden." It's all coming so plain to me, and nobody else in the park sees what I see, and it saddens me tremendously. The tears, man, I gotta tell you, they are clotting up my eyes, blinding me. Leonia, I am crying big tears for you. "Ho-ho-ho—look at that one, when the wind blows it, it makes the sound of aluminium foil crinkling, and the sound is knifing through the New Jersey afternoon—oh wait, look, that one's the sense of touch 'cause . . . I can *touch* it, kid!" And Clamor arches an eyebrow so perfectly, which is exactly what any normal *person* would do at this point, listenin' to me rappin', and I start laughing the hurtful kind. Too much. Those streaks of tearful depression are now glazed over by tears of joy, of abundance, of life, of companionship. And Clamor loves to see me laugh but hates to see me cry, so he licks the tears up quick, right off my face, and mauls me, kidding around, 'cause of the laughter. I'm even sending my dog mixed messages, you know?

But to make matters crazier, ascending over the family of trees is a cloud, shaped perfectly like a mushroom. Now, that could be a lingering remnant from World War II, or it could be a message from Leonia and/or God, like a silver sonnet co-authored, not giving me the secret to the universe, but maybe just waving to me—but waving hello or goodbye? And I pull my head back, like I did looking at the bus window, and the sky becomes graph paper, everything plotted out with exact coordinates, all objects neatly assigned its own minuscule square, giving even the vapors interrupting the blue an order, a reason, a purpose, a pattern. And I rest my knuckles on Clamor, mesmerized by the golden tufts of fur that peek through the spaces between my fingers. I can see the pattern to the atoms of his fur, and then even all the rows and mountainous coils of my own fingerprints. And the fire house looming large in its blood red, newly painted coat of bricks, is placed on the graph of God, and it all becomes simple, memorable, understandable. Heaven—a graph. Life—a graph. Once you know the plot of the planet, follow the formula of your soul, just pay attention. It all comes together easily—just do the math, kid!

And I take Clamor's face in my hands, and I study his eyes. Way up fucking close, I'm talking. I can see my own reflection in his eyes, and it's like looking into binoculars from the wrong end. Ever do that? I can see the world in his eyes, man, all the islands and oceans. Globes! Didn't I once say you were never supposed to look an animal in the eyes? Scratch that shit, man, you can look anyone anywhere, it's all a matter of what lesson you're after, at least that's what I'm thinking.

And off in the corner of the park, the weirdest thing is going on. There's this skinny guy like around my age dressed up in Elizabethan garb; I'm talking tunic, I'm talking tights, the guy's got the funkiest hat on, man, Robin Hood style, and he's got on like one of those skirts, or something. It's Hamlet incarnate, as far as I'm concerned. These shrooms are great, man, and I know this guy'll be good for something. If only Isabel were here with me. But in a million years you'll never guess what he's doing over there. He's extending his arms, eyes closed, and letting his breath out so, so slowly. Breathing exercises! This guy too? What's going on around here? I leave town for a little while, and all of a sudden everyone's doing breathing exercises? Do you think I should start doing those things? But I'm completely transfixed, and I probably would be even if I wasn't zooming, because this is just too, too fuckin' bizarre, man. And I'm looking over, and he surely would notice I was gawkin', except his eyes are closed, and he's completely into what he's doing, which is good for me. He's limbering up his lips, this guy. Man, these shrooms are getting me curious. I nudge Clamor and we strut over, kid—ready for anything, I ain't afraid of anything in this town, like I said. If he tells us to fuck off, we'll fuck off, or we won't if we decide not to—it's up to us, and no one's gonna tell us shit about anything.

We sit down maybe ten yards away from the guy, and for the first time I see that this guy has braids of shocking red hair spilling down close to his ass. I'm telling you, this guy is Elizabethan, for real. But wait a second—did people even have red hair back then? I don't know, man, I wasn't there. See? I told you I know when to defer. Did Eric the Red have red hair? You tell me. This guy, now, I think he notices us, me and Clamor, but he certainly doesn't nod or smile, I'll tell you that much right away. Maybe he's got an agenda. He flips open this little suitcase he's got—real beat up—and leaves it open, towards me. Then he swallows with great seriousness, and there is a tension in the park—what the hell is he gonna do, man? The "to be or not to be," maybe? Probably. Is he some kind of political nut? Hope he ain't a Bible-spouter, that ain't what I need to hear. Oh, let's hope he's not a mime. But, come on, I wouldn't be surprised about anything with this Elizabethan dude. So, he's kind of focusing and concentrating on the inside of his gut; he touches his stomach softly, as if it's vibrating or something—and if he happens to be shrooming too, I know it is vibrating, 'cause mine still is—and he moves his hand slowly from the stomach to the chest to the throat and then to his lips where he kisses two of his fingers gently, and then to the sky, hand shaking, man, shaking with passion. And from this little character comes a thin line of animal song, a razor of a melody, and it channels through the air to nestle itself into my ears and chime like heaven's harps plucked by the fingers of the saved. The voice comes from somewhere that I've never been, and I'm visiting it, and I want to stay there forever, until the implosion of the galaxies, and then maybe one more night. The notes in the voice are actual matter— like sugar, like cobblestones, like a praying mantis, like the face of the ocean. The lyrics drip out of his voice like the first droplet of brewing coffee plopping into an empty pot. It is a singular sound, preceded by black silence, and it is unable to be duplicated until the next pot of coffee. Until the next song. And my boy, Elizabethan boy, Hamlet, closes his eyes, and his hands start vibrating, way too fast for it to be a put-on, and his mouth is searching for just the right shape as if these are the last and only words in his vocabulary. He is where he was born to be, yet look at the pain. *"La donna è mobile,"* and I lean forward, my lips trembling, my eyes refusing to blink or twitch, unable to believe that such pro-fane beauty can exist on this planet, unable to comprehend that five years ago, my friends and I probably would have beaten this guy up real bad, or at least laughed at him. Guy, I cannot fuckin' fathom that peace and purity can even exist around me these days. And of all the messengers, man, damn. My world collapses and a new one is reborn immedi-ately. A better world, trust me. The singer puts his thumbs together, palms down, fingers stretched all the way out, a show of attempted restraint. *"Qual' piuma al vento."* Since my ex-girlfriend sent a bullet into her wide open mouth, I have heard the good Lord. I have heard Satan. I have heard voices call me with words of confusion and webs of indiffer-ence. God or the devil, who is responsible for this beacon? Leonia, where are you today? Can you see this glorious ruby shine? And the opera singer now cups his hands together, begging you to understand not the words, but the feeling; or maybe the feeling of having such a feeling. And the anticipa-tion of the next line lasts a perfect eternity, long enough for me to think of Pete Townshend. Are the words enough? Will the words be enough for the opera singer? *"Muta d'accento e di pensiero."* He sings it with a mournful, knowing smile that colors the note, just like, I got to admit, the expression of pain on the face of the leader of the Mulligans. But this guy; he is Rigoletto, the court jester. He's the Duke of Mantua, the Prince of Denmark, Jesus, Townshend, the unknown soldier. Pretty Leonia. He dresses up in that tunic in broad daylight, in public, because, my friend, he has something to say. And I shake my head, unable to comprehend what I'm doing on the lawn, and I stare down into my lap—I'm sitting Indian style—when's the last time I did that?—and begin to cry and cry as the tempo of the tune increases, the tears finally coming free like glorious poetry, like clever graffiti, like art that is there for you when friends are gone.

And out of habit or fate or accident, I graze my pocket—on the hip this time—and the back of my thumb hits my harmonica, which I had forgotten all about. I dig in there, and take that thing out, unable to see it because the tears are busy creating vague, moist circles of fog in my eyes. Groping around with it, I look through my tears at the opera singer. He looks like a blurry red demon. I position the harp up to my face, right where it needs to be. As delicate as you can ever possibly hope to know, I rest my lips on the edge of the harp. I know I can paint with the same color he's using. I know it. I whisper into my instrument, and as his voice of platinum seeps into the ozone, my swirling harmonica envelops every syllable with transparent wrapping paper, adding to it, but never, never covering it. His notes and mine disappear into the shadows of the sky to make love gently. It is perhaps the first time in my life I have acted without introspection, without self-consciousness, without doubt. I behave,

I don't act, and that's all the difference. Does my sister know the difference? And when the song ends, maybe three weeks later, it seems, I look up at him with adoring eyes, and he allows himself a closed-lip smile (mournful, still) of gratitude and grace. He mouths the words "thank you, thank you." I am trembling, because, I mean, I don't like opera, I'm telling you the truth, but I think I finally know how a woman feels when she gives birth to a beautiful baby. Damn, that ride home from the hospital—you're tired as anything, but I bet you're flying, still. It's religious, it's sexual, man. Sex. Religion. What's the difference? One gets peddled on street corners, and with the other, all you're worried about is the second coming.

My pesky peripheral vision picks up Isabel, sitting close by, barefoot in the grass, leaning on her elbows. Was she there all along? Must have been, because she, too, is weeping uncontrollably. The opera singer looks at Isabel, in character, and I know he's looking at her as if she was the embodiment of the mystery of women. He bows gallantly. Isabel shakes her head in defeat, overcome by the moment, and is now in complete shambles. I crawl over to Isabel, and we hug, weeping into each other's shoulders. And I cry for opera, I cry for art and Giuseppe Verdi, I cry for my hometown, and Wood Park. Oh, I cry for my sister, who I want so desperately to connect with, but she left me about an hour ago for her friend in the drama department, which really does hurt. Most of all, I cry for sweet Leonia, and how much I hate that she's dead and gone, because I did and do love her so much; you truly have to believe me.

"Women are fickle, like a feather in the wind, changing their words and their thoughts." I'm an Italian immigrant's son, man, I know what those words in the opera mean. But somehow, I could be the son of an alien or a caveman, and I'm telling you, I would still know what those words meant. I'm sure Clamor knew, I'm sure all the blades of grass knew. Italian has nothing to do with it. The opera singer again relaxes his shoulders, rotates his head around his neck, does some more breathing exercises. And I let go of Isabel's hand, which I had been clasping onto for dear life so the moment would not end. As if that were possible. I walk over to the opera singer's suitcase, and I look the beautiful opera singer right in the eyes, the way I do with most people. But the difference is that this time, I'm not worried about control, or intimidation, or fear, merely connection. I reach into my pocket and gently remove my harmonica again. My hands cradle it with love, blow one final note of thanks and hold the instrument out in front of me, release, and let it drop into the suitcase. It hits with a low loud thud, but that's okay. Times like this, man, there's just nothing to say, no words, trust me. But I'm not going to just leave, so I say as earnestly and as respectfully as I can, *"Grazie, signore."* Oh, does it come out soft, like the manner of my harmonica. Dude, I wish I could sit you down and spend hours, all through the night, telling you how sincerely I meant that. Again, he smiles shyly, like an awkward angel, and closes his eyes. That is our interaction, and I will allow him to return to the genius characters of his creation. I cluck to Clamor, and haul up Ms Isabel, and we're outta there.

The three of us walk slowly through the familiar yet different scenes of my hometown. Izzy and I talk to each other, really seem to talk this time, about law and logic and morals, the details of which just don't matter—it's not worth going into—we didn't really shed any new light on anything, except each other. Talking philosophy or psychology or any kind of abstraction is only good when everyone involved in the conversation is equally enthusiastic. And I was right there with Isabel and her theories about things. When I decided to come back to New Jersey, I never thought that it would be this great, me and my sister, toasty and heavy-headed from the mushrooms, overwhelmed by that Elizabethan experience, yet afraid to talk about it with audible words.

So we just walk down the main strip of town, and there's a bunch of people out, man, but nobody really looking at anyone else, if you know what I mean. People are content just to get from point A to point B on the graphs of their agendas, in a way. See? Content—I told you! So check it out, there's this pudgy guy who looks really Irish, fuckin' red face, with this little plaid fanny pack around his waist. He's sort of limping, so I don't know if he's lame, or a veteran, or an old time soccer hero—you just can't tell with this guy. Better keep an eye on him, right? Could be interesting. I nudge Izzy, and point him out. She locks in on him, man; that's one of the things I love about my sister. Even if she wasn't on shrooms, if I tell her something's worth it, she ain't gonna dispute it, she'll take my word, for the most part. And my man is hobbling along a little, with his red face, and just then like seven kids on roller blades blaze by us and the Irish guy, no problem. But maybe ten seconds after, we hear these shricks by this one littler kid with midnight skin, "Get the fuck out the way, muthafucka!" And he is movin', tryin' to catch up to his boys, and he bumps the Irish guy real hard, so that Redface stumbles out of the way and somehow just manages to regain his balance right before he goes down in a big way, ass first. The little speeding black kid is now a dot on the horizon, but the noise of his cackle in the distance is as chilling as any gunshot. Clamor gives a concerned bark, but the little kid is long gone. Now, understand, I'm even a little shaken up, and I was a good five yards away on the imaginary grid of the sidewalk. The Irish man, on the other hand, is all but hyperventilating, doubled over, face now fuckin' pure maroon. I call out to the guy, feelin' so sorry for him, wishin' it was me, 'cause I can handle things like that, kid.

"Sir, you okay?" What? No big deal. I can ask him, right? That's okay to do. He turns to me quick, flustered as shit, and his face morphs into a shade of burnt sienna. I broke him out of his private world of embarrassment and put him on stage in the theater of ridicule. I didn't know I was going to do that, didn't mean to, wasn't my intention. I asked him as a reflex, I swear to you. He looked just as startled that I asked him as he did when that punk ran into him. Yeah, man, now I get it, I've been there—it's bad enough that something like that happened, never mind someone else noticing and commenting on it—Jesus, is that the pits. Then, the strangest thing happens. He sort of shakes his head quick, like Clamor when he comes out of a lake, or someone waking up from a vivid dream, and focuses now not on Isabel and myself. He looks, though, in our general direction, and speaks. Speaks in a clipped, nervous, childish, tight voice, with an accent undefinable.

"Should have kicked that fucker's ass." And his words, like the opera singer's, evolve into visible entities, but these are vicious red lasers that pierce the air and glow against my chest. The hatred and venom are as foreign and unexpected as the potential beauty of opera was earlier. The sheer kinetics of it all, man, I wish you were there. And again, the Irish dude puffs out his chest, like a defiant infant, like a challenged animal in the jungle. And believe it or not, he adds with a new tone of assurance, accentuated with a nod, "Coulda done it, too."

And I just stare at him, man, disbelieving. I see so clearly the plan in his mind. Fight violence with greater violence. That's a mathematical formula right there, kid. Solve a problem with anger; it just makes me crumble. And I watch the Irish guy walk away, now satisfied with the recent turn of events, face saved, because he believes he regained my respect. He believes I believe him. He's totally lost, man, when it comes to me. When the initial instinct of sadness and pure wonder at the bewildering ways of human beings subsides, I look to Isabel; she is excited about the whole thing. So am I. Connection!

"That was *extraordinary!* He made sure we knew he wasn't scared, even though he obviously was. What did he care what we thought?" Man, Isabel was enthusiastic in a big way—this was like the girl I knew from old times. Better yet, she saw exactly what I saw. "In some way—" and like an untrained actor, or a bad friend, I stomp on her lines, giggles in my voice.

"Wait—Izzy, Izzy, let's examine this. He only acted that way because we were there, right? That's so strange. Think of Clamor. It's so beautiful—he would have acted the same way."

"What do you mean?" And she's dying to hear my explanation. And, believe me, I'd tell her, but I'm stumbling down various avenues of thought. Nothing coherent is coming out, 'cause there's so much to say, so many different words, so many millions of options to reverse and regret within each sentence, man. All the choices seem so seductive, so appealing, man. I just want to explain it all to her, bit by bit, no matter how long it takes. I am so frustrated. No wonder my man fucked up on the verbal section of the SATs, because there's just no way to make sense of it all, you gotta believe me. Think of it for a second—for every letter you use in everyday speech, you're leaving twenty-five perfectly good ones somewhere by the wayside.

"Isabel. When Clamor pisses on a stop sign, he lifts that leg *way* up there, so the other dogs come by and check the marker, and think he's larger than he really is. Why did that guy puff his chest out? Same reason."

"So you think it was some kind of primal thing going on? Like prehistoric?" Ah, now we're playing Q&A, just like it's always been. She's the Q; I'm not. I don't mind asking questions most of the time, but for some reason, when it comes to Izzy, I like to answer.

"Don't you see? We can't blame him at all. His father would have done that, his father's father, and so on, and I mean way back when man walked on all fours. We just saw the eternal discord of civilizations acted out before us. We saw boxing, we saw a world war, we saw the clash of the titans. Even if it was just that pudgy guy and some kids on roller blades." And Isabel is doubled over. I gave her a good laugh, her mouth is fuckin' *wide* open, no sound comin' out, and I'm laughing too, but not 'cause what I said was funny, 'cause it wasn't meant to be at all, but because my sister is laughing so damn hard. Real laughter, like real sadness, is infectious. Real anything is infectious, if you stop to think about it. That's true, but the only problem is, how many times a day do you get to see anything really real?

We are, I imagine, quite a sight, laughing like this, hugging, leaning on a blue mailbox, that happens to have the words *"Fuck You!"* etched into it. But here's the thing: it's not written in there with the poison that the Led Zep fan wrote his graffiti with back at the cemetery. It's sort of satirical, almost a parody of vandalism. I don't know, maybe a little kid did it just to be cool, or to be admitted into a club. This one I can laugh at. The Led Zep thing in the cemetery was over the line, man: difference. That was written with a snarl. This "Fuck You" was written with a smirk. Still puzzling, still don't get it. Wait—hang on a sec! Yeah, man, now I get it! The Irish guy, Clamor pissing, this guy who wrote the graffiti—exactly the same, man! All they are is marking territory. They are filled with an inherent inadequacy, and all they want to do is be noticed, be respected, be able to affect their surroundings in a concrete, tangible way that they can point to. Hey, maybe everyone is—all of us. Man, it all comes together sometimes; that's the fun of it all.

We get ready to cross the street, and this is the topper. This old girlfriend of mine, Nicole, is talking to some sausage of a traffic cop across the street, right where we have to go, man. What a downer. An old girlfriend? Shit, I hate small towns, I really do. I mean, first off, don't you wonder why I would ever date a girl named Nicole? What was I thinking? She's okay, I guess. I gotta say, I think about her sometimes, and get that little hollow feeling. She's a good girl, but I don't need to talk to her at all at this point. That's not up on my wish list in the least. I'm convinced the only living organism more disgusting than the cockroach is the ex-girlfriend. Interestingly, Leonia and I never broke up—don't forget that.

"Shit. Izzy, that's Nicole over there. Remember her? Don't say anything."

"Oh my God! She looks *so* good! Go talk to her, don't be a child. Just go." And you know what? While I'm so busy trying to play the older brother, it totally slips my mind that Isabel is a pretty smart girl, more grown up than I give her credit for most of the time, and she can come up with a reasonable idea once in a while. She's totally right, in this case. So I slip into a role—Isabel does it all the time—and pace over there with my thunderpup and my sister, feelin' good, looking forward to disrupting the cop. Do you think he'll be able to tell that I'm on mushrooms? Nah, there's no way, kid.

Suddenly, Nicole turns our way when she hears the jingling, and she notices me first, and her mouth opens into a big O, and her eyes widen, and good God, isn't anyone real anymore? She squeals for some reason, and gives me a big hug, which feels good. The cop excuses himself, which also satisfies the shit out of me. Yeah, *you* move on along, punk, I'm stayin' here. I hate authority, man. And for some reason, Isabel starts right in talking to Nicole about Clamor before I can even get a word in, and the three of them start making noises, and I am the observer. Now, I know it may just be the shrooms, but I can see so plainly how nervous and uptight Nicole is being, and how fuckin' fake Isabel is being, which she really doesn't have to be, and how in love Clamor is with the unexpected attention and affection. But I can't stand people acting stupider than they really are, so I gotta go. After a minute or so, I give them a wave, and take

Clamor with me. The two girls with artificially reduced IQs give looks of exaggerated disappointment, but I can't tell whether they are upset about me leaving, Clamor leaving, or that they're going to be stuck talking to each other alone. But that's a worry for some other day, because Clamor and I are jangling up Magnolia on our way back home. There's a huge racket as two squirrels chase each other up a tree, in that kind of frenzy where you don't know whether they're fucking or fighting—back to that whole thing about love and hate—and Clamor and I, protecting each other and ourselves, both immediately turn our heads the exact same way, the exact same speed, and at the exact same angle. Isn't that kind of cool? Peripheral vision again, son, I can tell. I feel way closer to Clamor than I do to Nicole. She wouldn't have turned her head in the exact same way I did, like Clamor. That was special.

But with Nicole, here we go again, that same Amtrak train in my head is goin' down hard, my hair whipping back, and I'm holding on for dear life. That girl, I mean, I went out with her for a few months, a long time ago, it's not like it should still be so fake, right? Especially after the guy and the opera, you'd think that would really be a turning point for me, but no, not at all. It's the same insecurities, gonna snap their jaws at me forever. And here I thought coming home was going to solve some of my problems. Who knew ex-girlfriends were gonna cross my path? I simply had no idea. And Leonia ends in a gunshot; Nicole ends in a silent treatment. Michelle, my Michelle, ends up a name, a memory, and a story that only means something to me. And everyone I know tells me I'm cynical when it comes to love. Mom, Dad, they like me but they can't talk to me. Isabel, she'll talk to me, but only on mushrooms. Are any of those scenarios what you would call love? Man, that Amtrak train is plummeting in the worst way, and thoughts of miscellaneous females ring in my head, snapshots of old girlfriends, the same pictures, pasted into the scrapbook of my soul. Yearbook pictures, the one of Leonia. And I can see all the smiles and first-date laughs slipping into tired, annoyed, hate-filled sneers, eye-rolls, and then ugly smirks, all accentuated by a backdrop of screams. And, for the dozenth time at least today, those tears plague the corners of my eyes again, and I try to think of an old girlfriend I can call up and talk to in any kind of civil way. I try to think of a friend, even a pleasant acquaintance that's a woman. My kingdom for a fuckin' x chromosome that I can connect with when I want to. Do I even know how to deal with women in the first place? I mean, I must know *something,* certainly more than the sausages, right? Trust me, Michelle basically had her pick that night, and she chose me. It ain't because I'm something so special to look at or anything. Then why did she do it? And when you're done with that stab at an explanation, why did Nicole freeze me out for all this time, and while you're at it, why did Leonia send me the Hallmark card that woke up the neighbors?

Dude, I'm not trying to push the responsibility on you, it ain't your headache; it's just stumpin' the shit out of me, and I've got nowhere else to turn. But if all the girls I ever had a thing for want me out of their lives, then Leonia and Michelle did it the right way; they made sure I was never going to see them again. Nicole, I can always take her on face-to-face. It's just that until a few minutes ago, I never thought I wanted to. And I don't want to; I must. I got to get this train turned around. But now that it all comes down to it, I got to ask the hardest question of all; do I even know how? And if you've been listening to me all along, you know I can bluff my way through just about any crisis I want, just explain it away. But you got to call me on that from now on, okay? Don't let me fool myself anymore. If I wanted to be lame about it, I could just invoke the theory of some dead psychologist and say that Nicole was all fake and distanced 'cause she still cares, and it's just that she couldn't express it. God, is this yet another thing that I can write off as the difference between love and hate? Listen to me, man, what a fuckin' cop out. Here I am, lecturing, telling myself that the difference between love and hate is irrelevant. That reminds me, I knew this guy whose older brothers used to beat the shit out of him all the time. And when he'd go cryin' to his mother, she'd always say, "They do that because they love you." You believe that shit? Some lesson, right? Yeah, kid, go ahead, treat people you hate the same way you treat people you love. And then do me a favor—God, I got to get this train steadied—see how fuckin' far that gets you. If I'm doing my math right, probably about as far as it's gotten me.

IV

OBJET TROUVÉ

And wouldn't you know it? It's fuckin' High School Part II, the Return of the Baffled, and it's all my fault, because I find myself dialing the goddamn rotary telephone in the dank basement, sitting at my dad's desk. Well, nothing's coming of it, 'cause it's six digits, and then a long pause with thoughts crashing around, and then I hang up quick. I mean, this is like when I used to try to ask girls out in high school, if I ever bothered, that is, with the dialing of the girl's number only part way. Then I'd suddenly think of something, some bizarre reason why I had to hang up, and then *Clicksville,* kid! Damn, I mean, what if Nicole's ma answers, or her older brother, or, worst of all, her herself? I got no rap at this point, I got no charm, I'm coming off an up and down mushroom trip, and I'm just sitting at Dad's desk in this freezing cold basement—no carpet for some reason—feeling thirteen again, tops, and that's clearly not the remedy. So I'm six digits deep for the millionth time, and I think again of the echo of the gunshot, how everyone in our apartment building must have sat up straight when they heard the bang, or definitely stopped and wondered. The Big Bang Theory.

And I'm thinking all these thoughts, reviewing and re-playing, and here in the basement I just must not have no-ticed, must have just gotten careless, but my mind had to have wandered as I dialed the final "2" that would put me through to Nicole, maybe even connect me. I mean, I guess I did dial that "2" without realizing it because I can hear the baritone drone that means you rang up someone else's phone, whether it was a good idea or not, and my right wrist twitches, like I better hang up real quick and go back to New York City to call it a day. But, man, I'm the type of person that once it starts ringing, I let it ride. I'm not out to crank people. I mean, what if they can trace it, or something like that. Listen to me—trace it. What is she, an ex-girlfriend or a CIA agent? What's the difference, come to think of it? Basically, one knows everything about you; the other carries handcuffs. Ah, fuck it, but the ring is interrupted, and the receiver gulps a click, and I can hear the TV on in the house—some laugh track goin' ballistic; is anything ever really that fuckin' funny? And then the tender, spontaneous Nicole, finally, "Uh-Hey-Lo?" Accent on the "hey." A giggle permanently lodged in her voice box, the toss of her top-40 hair that comes through in the added syllable, and, if I know the first thing about her, the phone expertly buried between her shoulder and her ear, while her hands do something more important.

Oh, Nicole. I miss the way she is—the way I know she is—way the fuck down deep. That wasn't really her before, with the cop. You're gonna think I'm nuts, but the way she answered the phone, that word—it's not even a word, her greeting, but the way she said it—made me remember why I fell in love with her. And I totally did. Even if I never defined it that way back then, kid, I'm telling you I can clearly identify love in retrospect. And if I'm not careful, I'm going to do it all over again. I guess that's quite a statement, that back in high school I used to *love* her, and, let's face it, that's not what I called her to discover. Boy, am I ever sorry I harshed on her before. It's my instinct to hammer people sometimes, maybe before they get me first, but I really should quit doing that. Stop me next time you see me doing that, would you? Tell me if I go too far. I mean, have I been drilling Leonia all this time? I hope not, I don't mean to; you gotta understand, that's not the point of this whole thing. Man, that would make me really sad. And this time, on the phone, Nicole freezes me out again, or rather, if I'm not going to throw blame around, I guess I freeze out my own damn self. Silence. Should I hang up? Is it too late? Fuck! Is she tracing my ass? "Hey-low?" Again. Wait one second longer, and you lose. There must be a difference between love and hate, because I do not hate Nicole at all. Maybe myself, but not her. I clear my throat. I close my eyes and try to have whatever Greek God of Schmoozing they used to worship way back when coat my skin with gilded, fraternity charm, sausage charisma, if you will. Then I catch a glimpse of myself in the reflection of the golden rim of Dad's desk blotter, and I shake off the notion, I shake off the purpose, and become Mister Mystery, trying to solve my life using the same fuckin' ten-dollar phone I played around with when I was four. You want mystery? Here's the case: me holding the receiver of my dad's rotary; a half mile away, Nicole and her good mood and manner and her cordless. My kingdom for a clue.

"Nicole? It's me." Nice save! The fewer words you say, the less chance the person you're talking to has an opportunity to know that you're scared, that you're lost, that you're

the brakeman frantically flagging down that barreling Amtrak train with the villain puttin' brilliant Gordian knots of
barbed wire around the ankles of the damsel in distress,
tying her to the tracks for good, 'cause when was the last
time you saw a hero around here?

"Sweetie! Oh my God! Mom, guess who it is!" What was
I trying to prove by the phone call, I mean, could I have
possibly made a bigger mistake? I don't want to listen to her
talk like that. But she has something I need. She has answers.
Dude, I forgot to ask you, as a favor, could you feed me a
question or two? By the way, in case I ever call you, and I
may, kid, do this for me—please don't fuckin' talk to people
in your living room or whatever when I'm sittin' there in my
house with the phone sticking out of my ear to begin with.
You think I like listening to half of a conversation I didn't
even call up to hear? I swear to God, I'd rather you just hang
up on me and call me back when you're ready to carry out a
conversation, one-on-one. Yeah, one-on-one. That's what I
need from someone, preferably a girl. Someone who's not
afraid to deal with me just as a person, you know? How is it
that Michelle doesn't mind giving me what I need right out
of the blue, and this one won't? Alcohol, maybe. Timing is
important, I guess. But this chick Nicole is driving me insane, squealing on the other end, just like she did when I saw
her on the streets, and she's acting like I'm Ed McMahon,
calling her to tell her she's a millionaire, which I think she is,
in fact, or at least her pop is—he's an inventor, something to
do with alloys, to my understanding.

"Yeah, Nicole, are you doing anything tonight—I mean,
do you have like half an hour or an hour free?" It's weird,
but something about the mushrooms makes my voice grog-
gier, deeper, maybe more intelligent. I can hear every conso-

nant reverberate through the walls of my brain. I savor every passage of wind through my mouthful of teeth and the cavern formed by my lips. Oops. There's a long pause. No reply. Shit, did I blow it again? Great, now my ex-girlfriends are going to stand my ass up? Join the club, Nicole. I sit completely still, petrified.

"For you? Certainly." She says this dramatically, which only goes to show that I ain't always in control. I mean, she did to me what I did to X-Man and the old lady on the walk who was fuckin' around with Clamor's name. Did it on purpose. She is in control. And now I remember that it doesn't feel so good when the coin flips. Dude, she had the cause to pause, and then she up and brought her point home packaged in lion's claws. As she had every right to do, but did she have to wait and let that lightning rod of self doubt electrify all the patches of my skin? Damn, she gave me a fit—where does she get off doin' that shit, asked the defeated hypocrite. Can I save face, now? Can I let her know I wasn't fazed by the mind game? Probably not, because I'll be talking and not even be believing it myself, which makes it unlikely that you can fool someone else, especially someone like Nicole.

"Cool. Cool. Can you meet me in the golf course at like ten? By the entranceway?" I pick a place closest to her house, so she's got no beef. We always used to meet there. I like walks. I mean, we always used to go on walks when we were going out, and also for a little while before that, mired in nervousness. And we wouldn't really stop to kiss all the time, not usually. We would talk about everything: high school, art, philosophy, sometimes—now that I think of it, mostly high school—and it was amazing. How come I didn't think of those things first when I saw her in the streets of my hometown? Do I really train my brain to think of only the bad, only the downward tracks, the tied-up damsel, the cackling villain with the tight mask, and the runaway train?

"For you? Certainly." She tried to play the same card twice, and this time it didn't work. She knew she had control by saying that phrase once, and she went once more to the well, and came up with piss-water and kelp. And both of us watched that shit fall short, so clearly, so obviously. Both of us heard the slight tremor in the voice, the same waver that I had. Now I know we're at about the same level of fear. And that doesn't really turn me on, make me happy, but it does make me look forward to seeing her, because I know I mean something to her, still, that she's not going to act like she did when I interrupted her with my sister and the dog. There's no doubt she can tell me things I need to know, and tonight. And I'm feeling all my senses on fire, for some reason. I'm feeling she'll turn me into a man of insight. We gotta meet in the golf course.

"OK, Nicole, the entranceway. Like half an hour." And I hang up first. Does that put me in control? I love her, so I say, and now I silently challenge her to a verbal sparring match with no referee and an audience consisting of just the combatants? Listen to me go on like this, would you? In the boxing match of my imagination, I win the round 10–9, for the fool's gold belt and the tin-can treasures.

Actually, I just realized—I've probably been misleading you up until now. When I say "golf course," I don't want you to think of plaid-clad dentists with cellphones playing on plush fairways and thick greens. It used to be a beautiful, huge, eighteen-hole golf course when I was growing up, and it's just not like that anymore. No, the town had a referendum like fifteen years ago, and all the non-golfing citizens voted to tear that shit down and put up fifty or so houses instead. It was funny, because the town voted in favor of the construction like fifty-three percent against like forty-something. And those few people in favor caused the destruction of all this grass, all those trees, and part of a lake, even. Oh, and now there's a playground of asphalt, and now we have a lot more rich people who moved into town. Look at those property values skyrocket, man, right on; isn't this cool? I suppose all the people thought about was that since they don't golf personally, why should there be this big fuckin' distraction when there could be a big rise in big business. Fair enough question, but what about the animals, what about the land, I mean, there were a lot of trees that just got fuckin' ravaged, and for a while—like years—the golf course looked like some sort of suburban war zone. For a while, that is, until the pretty, anonymous houses lined up single file, one at a time, to beatify the town. And now all we have is Wood Park to play around in. Which I guess is okay sometimes, when you're in the right mood. But the best part of all is that they renamed this zone "The Hillside Inns," and no one in my town ever calls it that, even the people who live there. Isn't that a laugh? Fuck it—it was called "the golf course" when it was a golf course, it'll be "the golf course" even when it's a piece-of-shit housing complex.

So I take off out of the house, all in one motion—legs flyin', door slammin', farewellin'—like I always do when I'm on my way somewhere, and, unfortunately, there's just no way I can take Clamor with me this time. I know it's tough for both of us, and God knows Nicole wouldn't mind seeing him, but it has to be done because I don't want any distractions at this point. He was counting on coming, I can tell how hurt he is, but in the end I have to refuse. It makes me kind of sad that I get to call the shots, like that it's not fifty-fifty, but to be honest, I wouldn't want to subject him to the conversation that I think me and Nicole are gonna have. Least thing I can do is give Clamor a break. Who wants to listen to a couple of exes—*dos equis,* man—rehashing shit neither of them really remember? It always comes back to me becoming a character witness vouching for my former self, a confused kid I think was wrong, in retrospect, most of the time anyway. Who's arguing? I can't help it if we share the same motherfuckin' name. But Clamor, he's privy to a lot of shit, more than you think. I mean, when I came back last night, he came over and licked me, and then he looked behind me for Leonia. Those kinds of moments don't go away, man, no matter how much poetry you write, no matter how many sessions you have with some Harvard quack, and no matter how many other girls you're with who break your heart even more.

As I leave home base and make my way down the dead-end street, away from the sign and towards the live end, I don't turn around to acknowledge the inevitable spectators peering out the windows of my house. I just don't. I already know that Clamor and the family are looking out the window, brainstorming all the possible things I could do to myself at night. I could easily humor them with a smile and a wave, just to calm them down, but I have to stare down the frown of the night; I have to show the stars and the black sadness that I'm no sucker. You've got to prove it again and again. Plus, this is the character I'm going with tonight, and I can't just affect it on command. I'm no smooth actor. I got to come from offstage right smack to the floodlights in the middle of The Role. Pass the script. Ah, too late; I don't know my lines, I got no clue, but watch the bluffing begin, and let's hope the audience isn't looking too close up my sleeve.

And I'm walking down the blocks of my hometown, with all the silly denizens tucked into their houses. I'm a few minutes early, I think, but I'm already walking, dragging my stiff left leg along behind my body, which is on the move. And my head, man. I make a mental note that if my head feels this bad when I get back to New York City, I should call someone, like a professional. I know the bouncer was just doing his job, but something may be fucked up in there, for real. I kind of miss the jingling of the dog, which usually keeps my rhythm for me on walks like this, but I'm doin' okay by myself. Maybe Nicole will wear a big necklace or something, something that'll jingle in its place. I can't decide if I hope it's a gold heart or not. My medallion is snug; it ain't saying a word. I told you the whole deal with that chain, right, kid? *Inside.*

I enter the golf course, and I still have a few minutes to go until I'm at the meeting place, I think. I slow down a little because I can feel a car moving real slow, suspiciously slow, behind me, going like three miles an hour, maybe. I instantly assume that the joker at the wheel must either know me, or is just trying to fuck with me, or both, but with my peripheral vision, I can see—before the bastards can see that I see—two kids throwin' the weekly papers out of either side of some station wagon, the papers skidding across the driveways like they got castors on their asses. Shit, I don't like my groove being messed up, and I want this time for myself, to think a little bit as I walk over to Nicole. Streets are public places, though, I got no control. The dad at the wheel is reading one of the papers with the light on inside the car, letting the vehicle coast past me. Fucker *better* have been

looking out for me—I would have gotten flattened by that
machine, I don't give a shit how slow it was going. And the
crazy rhythms of the papers crashing grow faint, yet still so
clear, as they echo through the golf course and the buildings
and the night.

I'll tell you, I used to have a paper route, but no one
drove me anywhere, that's for sure, and it wasn't weekly at
all; it was every day after school, and I had to jog my ass all
the way up to every house, and put 'em in the door, in the
fuckin' mailbox, or right there on the mat, depending on the
preference of the customer. These little kids hitch a ride with
Pops, and all they're doin' is tossin', tossin', trying to see, I
bet, who can throw harder, who can hit more garage doors;
they don't give a shit. That's, like, *fun,* no problem. Ten,
fifteen minutes—job finished, and then go pick up your
check. Me, I had to deliver those fuckers in mint condition,
rain or whatever, so the people could frame the front page of
every issue. And I used to go early in the morning on Sundays, man—I used to love when it was all dark except for the
traffic light on Broad Avenue and Hillside. When the light
turned red, it was like the eyeball of an alien monitoring my
paper route. I used to pretend that I had to deliver all my
papers before seven in the morning, or else aliens would take
over my hometown. The salvation of New Jersey—Earth,
even—was up to me, you know? I know, I know—pretty
damn stupid, but it kept my head occupied; it got me
through the morning. I wasn't bad, though. I remember
skipping one house one time—my only complaint *ever,*
kid—and the De Lorenzo son of a bitch calls me up, and I
gotta go over there for damage control, and he goes ballistic
on me, like his own picture was going to be on the front
page, or he wrote the lead article in there, or something like

that. So I tell the bastard to hang on, and I sprint downtown to Garden State and use my own fuckin' money to buy the guy a paper. It was only a quarter, but you'd think I bought the guy a Mercedes, he was so happy. Man, I bet if I saw that prick tonight, he'd thank me again for that. But it feels good to remember that I had a job, a life, before Leonia, before Nicole, before I thought that girls were interesting and mysterious. I sure hope I have some new memories after it dawns on me that girls are not all that interesting after all. But it still gets to me, man, that I skipped that De Lorenzo house. What was I thinking?

And waiting right there in the entranceway for me is Nicole, her elbows locked, hands in jacket pocket, causing her coat to stretch out a little bit at the bottom. This vision, my friend, could be a Xerox copy of one that happened five or six years ago exactly, easy. She's standing under a streetlamp just like she always did, and she looks cold, like maybe she needs a hug. I wonder why she got there early, if she even did. Me, I suppose I'm always a little late. I don't wear a watch, kid, but there's no need—I know it's always about nine minutes past the time I should be where I am, if that makes any sense. But she does look great, with these amazing dark waffle tights on, and she looks the way she used to look when we were at high school football games, even—she was *always* cold those times—and when we would look at each other in her living room, waiting for her mother to get tired. And her smile catches the streetlamp, instead of the other way around, and there's nothing more to say, except I know it's the real thing. Real. Not the way it was in the middle of town. Not the way it was when we ran through our list of infamous last words and ugly clichés as we were breaking up in the hallway of the high school, after she told me to write her letters and keep in touch, and that she hoped we could still be friends. That's all offensive shit to a guy like me.

"Some things never change," Nicole says, pointing at her watch, shifting her weight from her heels to her tiptoes, as a nice way of greeting, and Nicole says it softly, sweetly, with love, I'm sure. It's true, man, she's got me there. I guess I came late. And I don't want to get into it all right now, because I know if we small talk now, it'll never stop, there'll be no way we can make any kind of meaningful connection. I mean, look at me and my parents when we're at the dinner table; isn't that enough proof right there? But no kiss hello, I noticed—talk about setting the tone, huh?

"Nicole, let's go this way." And I stretch out my left arm, open palm, the way I used to do it on our first couple of dates, to movies, and random high school parties and events. Actually, come to think of it, we skipped most of those. But this is not a walk for hand-holding or kissing, or arm-arounding; I'm just trying to guide her down some remote path, up a few hills, away from streetlamps, and all. So I end up putting the inside of my forearm on her far shoulder blade, which is not exactly a loving gesture, but she gets the point, understands now where I want her to go. Maybe I think that if I didn't steer her my way, we'd be wandering around all night, each going down our private avenues, and our paths wouldn't cross, not once. Shit, I regret not bringing along Clamor. He would have been good in a situation like this, and it's not like he'd be disrupting us at all. I should show the guy a little more faith, I mean, after all this time, and all. But let's face it, as far as the direction goes, if you're walking with someone else, and the main priority is conversation, it doesn't really matter where you go, does it? Trust me, we're not going to be sightseeing, we've seen all this shit before. And plus, like I said, it's only ugly houses anyway.

"Oh, it was so good to see you today, and Isabel looks really great. She, uh, told me you guys were on some interesting substances earlier today," and Nicole chuckles. "I remember you always said you wanted to try that stuff." Shit, Isabel. My conclusion now is that she was doing the shrooms just to say she did them. Again, Isabel depresses me, man. I'm not trying to be Captain Trips over here, but I suppose my goal was for us to try to reach some sort of communal mindset or something, in a completely private way, and here my sister goes spouting off to the first person she sees, my ex-girlfriend or whomever, what we're doing. Now my only fear is that she might have somehow told the opera singer—man, I'd be really grateful if she didn't. He doesn't need to know. But the problem is, Nicole says it in this kind of phony maternal, tsk-tsk, judicial way, if you know what I mean, and boy oh boy, I just have to nip that shit in the bud, because I'm not out here freezing my dick off, trying to understand shit about myself, trying to come up with the right questions to fit with the answers I have—like fuckin' *Jeopardy!*—to listen to some ex-girlfriend talkin' the way she did this afternoon. I mean, how am I going to break it to her about Leonia if we're on two way different wavelengths? And she senses it, too, because the smile vanishes, and she looks, Jesus Christ, like a woman. Her face relaxes from the strain of fake smiles, and her shoulders lose their artificial propriety. She has those circular glasses, and I can't see the lenses, only the silver rims. I can see her slight frown of concentration, like she's thinking about something a little bit painful, like she's trying to pierce the annoying protective shield of conversation that every person has, certainly me, the goal of which is to keep other people as far away as possible. The question I have is: did anyone tell Nicole about the suicide? I mean, it wasn't in any paper or anything that I know of, but word travels fast in this town, or maybe Isabel blabbed about that as quick as she did that we ate those mushrooms. Nah, Isabel wouldn't want to bum anyone out, to have them associate her with bad news. She's okay, but she's a fuckin' baby, still, for the most part. But Nicole, the woman, sort of purses her lips a little bit, the expression you make when you really have something important to say, not just when you're making some fuckin' penny-ante observation, and she talks, in that distanced, thin voice I've grown to fear in people. "Before we get into anything else, I've decided there's something you should know." And a mercury beam of dread for some reason boils in my belly. Hmm. This isn't good at all. Did someone tell her?

Well, here it comes, I mean, the way she says that, her voice would have been the narration to the cemetery near my house. Now it's a real-ass conversation, and her graveyard voice just brings the chill of the night right into the pockets of my pants. My heart drops, and whatever moisture that was in my mouth is vacuumed right out of it, and I can only gulp, and maintain the role. And I stop. I sit down on the curb of the house and slap the concrete next to it. She sits where I slap. Man, is her ass as fuckin' blizzardy cold as mine? Don't worry, shit like that warms up, eventually. Either that, or you just end up forgetting about it. She looks into my eyes, frightened to tell me what she is definitely planning on telling me. I mean she is taking this mood, this vibe, so far, there's just no way she can withdraw now. The mushrooms, I do believe, have completely worn off now. A small dog howls in the distance. Nicole takes the deepest, thinnest, most feminine breath I can imagine.

"I know it's been a while since we talked, but I've felt like calling you every day since we graduated high school." Naw. Yeah? That was the last time, come to think of it, that we had seen each other; good point, Nicole, I hadn't realized that. Weird. "And there's a reason for that. I've asked enough people about you, and everything, and I'm glad we're finally face-to-face so I can tell you something." Man the way she's talkin', now I know—she *does* have a script. This is definitely rehearsed, but maybe she has some advice for me; who am I to refuse it? "Sweetie, I can't put off telling you this much longer. Look at me."

And with those words, that tone, it hits me like a slap to the face, wakes me up out of whatever dream I had been entertaining. I start to feel dizzy, because I think I know what she's going to say, yeah, I'm pretty sure, unfortunately; and the golf course starts spinning, and I realize my head's shaking, while my eyes dart to look away, down at a sewer grate, listening to the faint movements below. See, now Nicole *can* say anything, it's still wide open, but her manner has already told me—all pronouncing the words will do is confirm it. "I never told you this, but—" and Nicole takes a breath, and our forced eye contact is still hovering in concrete, and I know exactly the words she's going to choose, as events start piecing themselves together amazingly rapidly, like when you're watching some mathematician do a complex equation on a blackboard and he already knows the answer but he's just filling in the blanks so you can see it in black and white.

But the numbers fall into place so quick, man. I know

what Nicole is going to say, and I do everything but put my two hands on either side of my face so I won't let her down, so I won't look away. In the eyes vs. not in the eyes; the debate rages on: what is the tally up to now, have you been keeping track? Animals, ex-girlfriends, opera singers, bus drivers, sales clients; shit, kid, fuck it—look *everyone* in the eyes, who gives a fuck, let 'em deal with it themselves. And I know what Nicole is going to say; I'm absolutely positive, but I'm praying she won't. I am praying, praying she won't say what I know she's gonna say. No! Please don't say it! "Two months after we broke up, I had an abortion." And boom—there she goes, saying what I knew she would. No way I can explain how I knew, but take my word for it—somethin' about the tone of her voice—maybe you only talk a certain way when you talk about abortion. And the grids of the universe shatter like a golf ball shootin' through stained glass at St. Peter's. Another moment to chalk straight up to the devil, another unanswered prayer made several years too late, and another opportunity for me to try to withstand the echoes of the sharp-toothed cackling of Leonia, resounding from the ashes and the regal sea.

And check out Nicole, full of secrets, looks like she's closing her eyes, but she's really just looking down at herself, concentrating on her lower lip. She doesn't want to cry—she probably told herself earlier in the evening that she wasn't going to—which kicks your ass every time. You can't stuff those fuckers back in your eyeballs once they're created; they're coming out no matter what you do. Just let it flow. And her lips start trembling until it looks ridiculous, then they come steady, and then constant streams of water flow, expelling some of the poison from her conscience, but I doubt all of it. Some of that shit is forever lodged there, no question. She makes a horrible shape with her mouth, doing anything to get out one more sentence before the real floodgates open up, and she blurts a mass of vowels, "I didn't want you to know!" And for the billionth time in my life, my shoulders become sponges, soaking up teardrops and saliva and snot caused by the sadness of a girl, a girl that all I wanted, or thought I wanted, was to make happy, a sadness that I was pretty much totally responsible for. The devastation begins. Sorry—*continues*. And no waiting shoulder receives any of my falling teardrops.

And we sit there, embracing, shaking for the neighborhood, like we're breaking up for the first time, this time for real, because no tears were shed back then. Sadness postponed, hidden, becomes multiplied when it is finally uncovered. But a high school romance down the drain and a *baby,* man, a little kid, are two different things. I thought the ultimate sadness was seeing Leonia's life drained out on the tile of the bathroom, but that ain't completely the case, you see. With that, sure there was immense sadness, but there were so many other competing feelings: jealousy, anger, relief, admiration, and then the sadness creeps through. With this, what else can you feel? Sadness for Nicole, who deserved better than me, sadness for her mother, who must have been the support system in my absence, must have driven her to the clinic, and sadness for the little kid, with my traits and Nicole's innocence and beauty, and our combined nature transformed into a clump of blood and trash and nothingness on some operating table. And the tears flow.

In our silence, we think the same things, the same things lost, in chronological order, at the same time. We mourn the same things at once, which for her were years in coming. Me, I've been searching for a moment like this, where I can share true emotions with someone, but my own baby is a high price to pay. My spirit was staggering and now it's down for the fuckin' count. I remember this story my drunk old Irish Literature professor told us about Dierdre. She was forced to marry someone she didn't want to, so as she was being led away to the wedding, she dashed her head against some rocks. That was supposed to be the ultimate act of heroism and whatnot, her doing that. I can see that, 'cause Leonia chose her fate; admire her. Nicole chose someone else's fate; pity her. Both of those girls get me to thinkin' I have a heroine addiction or something, and I'm just strung out in some sewer, begging for an end to all the madness.

Listen, man, I'm begging you now, please don't start hating me over this. That's the last thing I need. If I were in your shoes, I'd be tempted to, too, but you can't. Trust me, it's breaking my heart to hold her like this. You're gonna start thinkin' bad thoughts about me, if you haven't already, but, man, you just gotta understand, this is a lot tougher on me than it is on you. You haven't walked a mile in mine, and, not that this excuses anything, but if I had one wish, just one thing, I'd ask that it never happened. And if it had to have happened, I'd ask that it happened to someone besides Nicole. Trust me, that's what I'd wish, like I said, if it means anything to anyone.

"Nicole, Nicole, please, why didn't you call?" See, that reads as being all accusatory, but it's really not. What else was I going to say, with my lame-ass, ad-libbing self? I'm just trying to tell her that I'm on her side, and I'd have been there for her if she wanted it. With that, if you want to take the opposing side on me, you're probably right, or at the very least you and Nicole sure see it eye to eye, 'cause she takes

her face off my shoulder, and turns right the fuck around on
me and looks my ass in the eyes. Right there, man, zeroes in
on the motherfuckers, you know?

"Oh, yeah? What good would that have done? Tell me
that. What would you have done? Chipped in half? Hired
me that limo to the clinic you'd always promised if it happened? It's your fault! It's your fault!" And she's right, of
course, and in the sparring match of our conversation, she's
wearing brass knuckles 'cause she's got the facts and truth all
the fuckin' way on her side, workin' for her, and I've got my
hands tied behind my back, and with every gasp for breath
and every syllable she barks into the crisp New Jersey night,
she's breakin' ribs, knockin' teeth to the sidewalk, and turning my cheekbones of ivory into powder, sawdust, and human debris. It's no contest, and she ain't stopping. "You got a
lot of nerve to ask me that question, as if you'd know what
to say. You'd probably have paid for the stupid blood test just
to make sure it was yours before you said one kind word,
one word of comfort, and you know that's true." Me too, I
know it's true, to a point. But *inside,* man. I know it's true
inside, not for the world to hear. "I don't mind you being
uncaring, well I do mind, but I can accept it. As long as you
don't sit there at a time like this and pretend you are. I mean,
that's pretty low."

What an eruption. A truly Leonia-esque display of anger.
But Leonia usually did it within. Like an iceberg, nine-tenths
of what could sink your ship with Leonia was hidden beneath the surface. But I'm warning you, I don't care who you
are, abortion or whatever; she's about to cross the line. She
says one more anti-me thing, and I'm coming right back at
her. I probably did fuck up—surprise, surprise—but I ain't

no sittin' duck. See, I could use the Leonia thing like a cannonball against the bullets of her abortion and make her feel worse, but you don't see me doing that, do you?

"I'm sorry," groans Nicole, and—boom—she buries her face in my shoulder again, and liquid exhaustion seeps out with every loud-ass sob. I think I was just on the receiving end of four years of resentment. You know, I think she really did set out to tell me as an ordinary statement, but the guilt and sorrow just came crashing down, and I'm crumbling, still; I'm lost. Two weeks ago, I would have told you that I might be a little out there, off the beaten track, maybe, but I'm certainly not capable of killing anyone. And not only, as it turns out, am I capable, but I am completely and totally one-hundred percent responsible for two lives, two beautiful lives, gone. Basically on my watch.

Nicole, who seems older and more of a hardened woman with each pace, has stood up and started walking up the hill, the opposite direction from her house, from the streetlamp that had framed her features for me so mystically. I walk behind her carefully, trying not to scuff my shoes or kick a pebble, trying not to interrupt the flow of her thoughts with my feet. More than anything, not to be trite, but I feel like a fuckin' idiot. I feel a million times more ridiculous than I did pukin' for all of the East Village to see. I feel so expendable and useless that I don't know what to do, what my arms are doing attached to my body, or why I bothered wearing clothes in the first place. I mean, it's a good thing I decided last minute not to wear that paper boy hat, or I would have really felt like a fuckin' clown. Tell me, man—why don't other people seem to make mistakes as bad as me? And the horrendous part of it all is that I realize this is yet another favor. Nicole having the operation and leaving me out of it for my own sanity is a favor—she didn't want my life to be complicated, and she shouldered the burden all by herself. She could have been a martyr; all she had to do was try a little harder. What, was she doing me a favor, or would I, in fact, have just been useless? And as Nicole gains a little speed and is now growing smaller in the distance, I think of what a sketchy operation an abortion is, so I look up to the unknown and say a silent prayer, sayin' please let the doctor or nurse, or whoever did the operation, please let the person have done it right, and not have fucked up Nicole's insides. And, as if she heard somehow, or knew what I was thinking, Nicole turns around and you can see the shine of the tears down her cheeks as if her face is shellacked in columns, and I'm afraid I already know the answer, 'cause there ain't no way her insides are as wonderful and pure as they were before.

The wind starts whipping up for the first time tonight, and I jog up to Nicole, not that I know what the hell I'm going to do when I catch her, and she slows down a little, allows herself to get caught, and I put my arms sloppily, maybe too aggressively, around her neck, so she's got to stop. She looks at me and shakes her head. "I think about it every day. There was just no reason." I nod, a lump in my throat sprouting like you wouldn't believe. I wonder what I did that day, the day Nicole had her abortion. The fear she must have had compared to me, as she laid down on that operating table with no pants on. Jesus, that day, I must have been making fun of people, out drinking with friends, maybe fucking someone else without a condom and deciding not to pull out, just like this whole Nicole business must have happened. And here I am, trying to come home and play myself off as the victim when there's a hollow girl at home, a dead baby, and don't forget the perfect girl in ashes. Nicole would have been a great mom, I don't give a fuck how the fuck old she was. She would have been, she's just that kind of person; you gotta know her, man. "Poor baby," she mutters. And, of course, I have no idea if she's talking about me, herself, or the unnamed baby. Probably all of us, or at least two out of three. I'm not going to ask her what she means, 'cause I can guess where she's coming from. I give her a look, the only one I got right now, that tells her I know that I really fucked up this time, and she produces the most sincere, beautiful, crooked smile, and her eyes shine, and they probably would have shone just like that even if she hadn't been crying all this time. You know, it has nothing to do with the water. What a smile.

And Nicole takes the final step to erase the space difference between us, and she gives me a hug, but totally not a loving, bear hug. It's more like she's softly wrapping her arms around my body, just far enough until her hands connect, and she keeps it there for a while. I told you she'd be a great mother. She, in effect, punished me, let me know how she really felt, and then comforted me, not to tell me that all was okay, but just to tell me that she did, in fact, love me at least in the nostalgic sense, and that I was still an important person to her. I just hope I'm not a four-letter word in her vocabulary, that if anyone mentions my name—not that they ever would—she won't wince, instinctively grasp her stomach or anything like that, but that she'll just maybe give a tired smile, roll her eyes in a show of ambiguous love, and the conversation can move on from there. I'd settle for that; I really would. I mean, I don't just want to be known as the guy who got her pregnant, even if it's technically true. Nicole releases her hug, which I sort of wish she didn't, and she reaches around to the back of my head. She claps it with the palm of her hand, squeezes, and keeps it there, so I'm talkin' she has complete control, nothing for me to do whatsoever. She pulls my face into hers and gives me a firm kiss right on the lips, making everything about me sparkle. I guess she notices, because she smiles wide, tears still roaming around her eyes, and, just joking around, I'm sure, she shoots her eyebrows up a little. Damn, she's still got it, man. And she puts her thumb and pinkie wide apart, sort of imitating a telephone receiver—although it looks more like my Pop's rotary than her cordless—which I take to mean that the walk is over, she's said all that has to be said (for now) and we'll talk on the phone soon, or at least that she wants to.

I'd tell you that it was a short walk, but I have no idea how long any of this went down for. Sometimes, we'd walk 'til sunrise, both of us shivering and happy. But she breaks away and slowly crosses the street, and just for a split second, man, just for an instant, she looks off to the side and I can see her profile and the way some far-off streetlamp seeks out the meaning of her eyes. And the vision is erased, replaced quickly with Leonia, and the cruel mystery has doubled, mitosed, multiplied, reproduced, and the answers I sought became camouflaged riddles and rhymes, with two legendary people in my life toying with the strings of my guilt. And tonight's meeting with tonight's puppeteer ends with me standing stunned on tonight's street corner, my thoughts and memories spinning, watching tonight's ex-girlfriend of mine fade into the distance, waiting in vain for her to return. And what do you think I'm supposed to do after an incident like that? Your guess is as good as mine, but if you think I'm going to another liquor store, or to check the *Voice* to see if the Mulligans are playing somewhere tonight, you're nuts.

And my thoughts swing to the gun in the bathroom and Michelle in the stairwell, but I shake that shit off real quick. I just can't subject myself to all that again, no matter how fuckin' bad the news is. This stuff just won't go away, I can understand that, I'm just sitting around hoping it won't get worse. Everyone makes mistakes, but I mean, Leonia, Nicole, I got to be straight with you, these were originally the nicest people you could ever hope to meet. Michelle. Now, Michelle with the gold heart, I wonder what I did to her, what disease I gave her, what kind of bad memories I've caused. What, pray tell, permanent damage have I done to Michelle? To you? I wasn't gonna say anything, and I know you're gonna hate me for this, and it's killin' me, but all I'm gonna say about Michelle is that—and I don't know what she had, or what the fuck went on in the way of details—but I certainly didn't leave my apartment that night with a condom. I'll tell you that straight off the bat. I'm not here to lie.

And the darkness of my mood dwarfs the literal darkness of the evening, and a dimly flickering streetlamp annoys the living shit out of me, grates on me big time, so I have to move on. I'm cutting through people's yards, ignoring the yips of tailored dogs and the yaps of rich homeowners. The night air thins out and the mercury drops, the wind causing the flaps of my dad's coat to draw closer, and a couple of my red fingers to search for more buttons to fasten, trying to do anything to stay warm. Clamor usually helps me keep pace in a situation like this, especially when I have a lot of stuff on my mind, so I have a feeling I'm going really slow. I reach a cul de sac which is right below a small patch of trees, a wooded area that the construction people must have spared, tossin' a bone to enraged citizens. Well, that's where I want to be. I want to be where I was when I was a kid, before

Leonia killed herself, before my son or daughter died, before
Isabel turned rotten, before I kind of fell in love with Michelle, and God Almighty do I love Michelle. It hurts to say
it, but it's true. So I vault this little wall, and I'm up in the
only wooded area around here. The dirt is hard, and when
my Timberlands pound on it, the sound is like from when
they pound on pavement. I look to a tree, off to my right,
and I see an empty fifth of Jack Daniels whiskey, and I
swear, involuntarily, my guts tighten up like a fist, and my
mouth opens, and my throat gags. I grin after I do that, even
though it hurt like all hell. I am proud of my body for
having that impulse; at least that's a start. Good, man, I'm
glad that's my instinct; that'll be the start of the new and
improved me. Well, not new, not improved, just soberer and
less dangerous to myself and others. A gray cat with M&M
eyes screeches and scampers after something it sees and I
miss. What a fuckin' racket, ma'. Cats.

You know, the last time I can remember existing for any
length of time without constant fights or constant trouble
was the time I spent in Italy. Man, I'd love to close my eyes
and have this become the Spanish Steps in Rome and have
my psycho cousin by my side, and just play music, play "Just
Like Tom Thumb's Blues," or something. Speaking of that, I
graze my ass, searching for the harmonica, because I know
that right now it would say something that I couldn't say in
English or Italian. Words fall short sometimes, I don't care if
you're bilingual or not. But, shit, I gave up my harp to the
red-haired opera singer in Wood Park, remember? Damn,
I'd love to have it back, but I wouldn't want that guy to
forget me, either. I don't know, what do you think—you
think he kept it?

And I walk over to the Jack Daniels bottle. There should

be a skull and crossbones on that fucker. I'm the cause of all my problems, but Daniels is the cause of all the exacerbations. And off to the side, as the gleam of the streetlamp oozes through the trees, I can see this little packet on the ground, buried under a thicket of a bush. I'm down, man, on my stomach, and I come up with the thing. I don't know why, man, I guess now I'm looking for answers anywhere. But this thing I'm drawn to. The answers to the pop quiz of the galaxy sure ain't at the bottom of the bottle, but who knows, they might be off to the side, like this here little packet. I flow over to the lamp's glow, and I can see that it's the perfect incident of suburban buried treasure—some sort of earring, like a diamond stud or something, some jewelry. Well, why did someone leave it here? Now, the outer package looks ancient, like it's been here forever. Maybe it's been here since the golf course was actually a golf course, before the construction workers redefined the town and our moods. Thing is, the earring is in excellent shape, looks great, maybe even unworn, with a different prism displayed with each angle I tilt it into the false sun of the lamp. And, yeah, it all fits into place—this is *my* earring from now on. *Objet trouvé!* Found object! Serendipity, motherfucker! That's just what I've been saying, man, the answers come exactly when the questions cease to be uttered. The answers confound the questioner, until the questioner shuts the fuck up and pays attention. They say the only stupid question is one that isn't asked. Bullshit! The only stupid question, and this covers most of them, is a question asked with no regard for the answer. And I need this earring *in,* man, even though I'm not really the jewelry type of guy at all. Let's face it, I keep that medallion buried near my heart, where no one goes at all. But I need this earring in, and I need it in now. And I don't know if what I'm going to do is being a wiseass or a best friend, but I know she's done it before; I know she can do it, and I bet she will do it, if I ask. Now my only question is: does Nicole even want to see me right now?

So, the rock pinched tight between my thumb and forefinger, I'm on my way to Nicole's—like a ten minute walk, no problem—and I truthfully don't give a shit about the consequences, whether her ma wants me dead, or whether her dad is up on the roof poised with a hunting rifle, waiting for me to show the whites of my eyes. The ma sounded kind of happy when I was on the phone with her daughter; she squeaked loud enough for me to hear. Actually, once again, I got no idea what time it is right now, but I would bet they're asleep. Here's hopin', but don't confuse that with carin'. And I leap off the little wall, the Timberlands landing hard against the asphalt, the shock buzzing up the backs of my legs, and I'm down the block on the way to Nicole's house for like the first time in maybe four or five years. Man, I can't believe my agenda became so irrelevant so quick. I was all ready for Nicole to help me on the road to recovery, but it's clear she needs to get on that road first.

When I get to the house, I stop right outside the driveway, touch my zipper to make sure it's up, wipe my nose; the same shit I did when I was a teenager, when I so desperately cared what people thought about me. Now, I still do, don't get me wrong, but there's also the realization that you really can't change people's minds once they get an impression of you. That's the essence of male maturity. There's just no use, man. I can bet Nicole's folks have a pretty definite opinion of me, that's for sure. The whole house looks really dark, except the lights of the TV set are dancing through the window, purple and orange, and lighting up the entrance to her backyard. Gotta be Nicole, thinking with the TV on—that's a good way to do it. That and staring in the mirror, I've found.

And I knock on the door real quiet, so only the people who are awake can hear it. I'm fuckin' cold out here, so I switch my weight from my heels to my tiptoes, anything for some circulation. The curtains on the front door spread, and I get a zoom close-up of her gobstopper eyes, kelly green with a rust-colored trim. And just like so many times before, my heart quivers, and the curtain closes, and after a pause about as long as the one on the telephone, when all my failures spring up for potential rekindling, three locks click loud, and the door cracks open. Nicole smiles with her eyes, like she's glad I dropped by—she wasn't expecting me, was she? She hugs me in the doorway, this time like she really means it, and I can feel the gray fleece of her pullover, and as we release, I can see the waffle tights still on, and I can smell the apricot in her hair, some of that organic shampoo, probably the same overpriced brand Isabel uses.

"Nicole. You gotta do me a favor." My voice sounds totally different now. Raspy and desperate, hurried and exhausted. I hold up the earring, and then I pinch my left ear lobe. It's funny, 'cause she sort of tilts her head at a little angle, like my boy Clamor does when he sees something he's never seen before. And after a second, it probably dawns on her what's up, and Nicole throws her head back, laughing. I didn't have to say much, and she knew just what I meant! Connection? What do you think?

I sit on the toilet, the seat down, and I look over as Nicole lights a match and holds it up to this long, thick sewing needle. That's probably a good idea—I want the earring, but who the fuck wants to get infected or something? What does that prove to anybody? And she puts the flame to the needle and the flame to the stud, and then blows the match out, sending thin wisps of smoke up to the ceiling. Nicole, man, you can always count on her for shit like this—I knew she'd do it for me. Lotta girls, man, you wouldn't even bother askin'. Lotta girls, they'd tell you to go to the mall, or a shop or something. Nicole knows me, or at least knows me well enough to know that putting the earring in means a little bit more than just accessorizing, you know?

"Thing about the ear, sweetie, there's two membranes. In the middle, all that's there is air, like a balloon." Nicole knows this shit? "So it's gonna be, like, pop, pause, pop, all in the span of like a tenth of a second. Quick and painless. All right?" I nod, excited and not the least bit scared. Fact is, I'm happy I'm putting her in a position where she can cause me some pain; that'll be fine. Let her operate on me for a while. I don't mind at all. Shit, I'd let Leonia pierce the other fuckin' ear, if I could. Let's pass the pain around. And here I am, fronting as the martyr, but I don't really know shit, because it's just a prick, like a tetanus shot or something—I only feel one, not two—and I look up at the mirror, and Nicole is squeezing the earlobe, the tip of her tongue sticking out the side of her mouth. I can see a thin stream of blood crawling a dark red river down the lobe onto my neck. "Ta-da!" and Nicole smiles again, a monster contrast from the way she was outside in the golf course, and we smile at each other's reflections. She releases my ear, which feels a little pressure, but no pain, and I can see the found fake diamond glinting at the base of my ear. I look away from the mirror, and she meets my eyes in real life, not in any glass, not secondhand or anything, and I offer her my hand. You talk about a connection, man, a moment, having some girl with a needle pokin' around in your ear will do it to you every time, no problem. There's been a lot, too many to count, but this has to be the best favor anyone's ever done for me. And I check my gaze from all sides, all angles. The new me? Yeah. New. Maybe even improved; you tell me.

V

REFUSE YER NAME

Hindsight is a million times better than x-ray vision any day of the week. Now, say what you will about whether or not I was just looking for trouble coming home, but I certainly didn't plan any of this shit—I mean, the mushrooms, the ex-girlfriend's abortion—none of that shit at all. Nah, that kind of snuck up on me big time. So is that what you're thinking, too, that this whole return home thing was a bad idea to begin with? Maybe; I wouldn't be surprised for a second if you're right. I mean, if you're going to second guess me, then I got no case. It has for sure not turned out to be the best odyssey of my career, but hey—like staying in New York City would have been any better? What's there for me there? Thing is, in my defense, it's not like I seek trouble, just more that I tend to attract it, like some devilish magnet. Somehow, I can be walkin' down the street, minding my own business, and boom—ex-girlfriend shows up. Then, I could be chatting with her on the phone, asking her out to a walk, just a simple walk, it's not like I had anything else in mind and, look out, she's got some of this other pretty hairy shit to tell me. Trouble all around and me in the middle of it. Come to think of it, whose idea was it for me to come home in the first place? I mean, no offense, but that wasn't too bright, was it? Since when did home ever have the answer? Out of the frying pan, into the fire and—whoops—sinking deep in the inferno. Sometimes, you think of something you did and wonder who the hell really controls you, because you wouldn't think to do something that stupid on your own. Maybe, thinking about it, I originally came home for some kind of spiritual reawakening, some kind of answer, a connection, maybe, but all I did was escape present failures and inadequacies to revisit the ones from the past, and those are even worse, 'cause they've had the chance to fester and set and become permanent—there's just no need for it. That's not going to do anyone any good. Man, that reminds me—I know this guy from school in New York City; he doesn't talk to his parents, doesn't talk to his sister, doesn't talk to any of his old high school friends. He thinks all that's doing is revisiting destructive relationships. I used to think that was hardcore and mean, but as it turns out, it's possible he's got the right idea; it could be. He figures they wronged him in the past, so he ain't gonna let 'em do it again. Now I don't think I'm going to go that far—all that doesn't really appeal to me, but I used to rank on the kid a little for that, and now I see more where he's coming from. Why talk to people if all they do is bring you down? Oh, but if we're going to play by those rules, I can tell you there won't exactly be a long line of people beating down my door for all my cheer and good conversation, you know?

I scoot down the stairs to the main floor, and Clamor's there for me. Just Clamor all by himself this time. See, it's easy to tell that this morning, the thrill is gone—no welcoming committee, just the dog. That's how you can tell your true friends, kid—stay home more than one day. What does it mean when your dog is your most enthusiastic fan? I guess it means you're on the right track. But Clamor always looks his best in the morning, with his coat framed in gold by the universal sunshine beating through the windows. I flip him a doggie cracker, just to make sure I stay on his good side— like Clamor has any other side—and he swallows and then splits. Good dog.

Now, I gotta tell you, I don't even have the newspaper open, I don't even have the first bite of a poppy seed in my mouth, before Ma barrels into the dining room and starts squealing about my earring. Holy shit! I totally forgot about the earring, and Ma starts fiddling with it, telling me how red it's getting, but that I look good, that my face was made for an earring, whatever that means. She's not really a jewelry type of person either, but that doesn't mean she doesn't know when something looks good. Damn, having your mom's approval really takes the fun out of getting an earring, doesn't it? Especially when she starts twisting it around, and smearing rubbing alcohol all around it. There's just no need for that; it's not going to get infected or anything. I mean, Nicole did sterilize it, didn't she? That *is* how you're supposed to do it, with the flame, right? I'm telling you, when I woke up in the morning, I didn't even feel that earring in there, but once Ma brings it up, it starts throbbing a little bit, and I can feel the burning inside. I can just picture the way the needle of the stud pierced every molecule of fiber in my skin, and it's all just kind of sickening.

My bagel starts to taste a little like rubbing alcohol fumes, so I pull my head away from my ma, and beg her to stop. Not missing a beat, man, she starts in on me about sticking around just for today (at *least,* she says) and that I gotta go check out Isabel's matinee performance today down at the high school. She tells me I can go home after the performance, but it means a lot to Isabel that I see her being Juliet. I knew this was gonna happen, I swear. I should have known there was no way I could go home without seeing that thing. I knew I was going to get sucked into drama sooner or later, like it or not. All I wanted out of this weekend was less drama than in New York, and it's been just the opposite. Man, I know she's my sister, but what's the point? I don't really like plays. The only thing I know about plays is what I learned in high school, which is that supposedly Aristotle once said attending a play requires a "willing suspension of disbelief." Oh is that so? Well, guess what? I ain't willing to suspend *shit!* And I'm not totally into paying to watch Isabel act when I can do it for free anytime I want. I saw a damn command performance yesterday, didn't I? Some kind of serious actor she is, man, the day before a performance she's off doin' shrooms like there's no problem. Come to think of it, it'll probably improve her performance, if she took enough of them, that is. Like I said, I definitely took more than she did, had a longer trip, I think. But who's keeping track; what kind of pettiness is that?

But remember what I was telling you about spending my whole life just takin' favors from people? Yeah, that's really how it seems lately. I mean, when they don't just go ahead and *do* 'em for me, I'm tricking other people into doing exactly what I want them to do in the first place. A lot of times, it's pretty easy—no problem. But I mean who really does a favor if they don't eventually want something back in return? Now, with Ma, I've got no problem doing her a favor, or even Isabel, but this play thing isn't totally what I had in mind for today. It seems like sitting in a seat for three hours isn't going to do anything but make me an easy target for the spears of my thoughts, and one of them is bound to get me dead center, and I'll be done for. This play, now, trust me, I could get out of it, it's not like I can't think of anything to say, but sometimes shit like that is more trouble than it's worth, and more often than not, you just end up hurting people's feelings. Dad is usually off playing tennis all day on Sundays, and then watching one of the football games with his friends. Have you ever noticed that once you're through watching a football game, nothing's changed at all, except you're three hours older?

So with Dad out of the picture, this could clearly be a me-and-Ma type thing. And you know I got no problem with that. Eating a bagel, reading the A section, I tell her that I'll go, and she smiles and tells me that Isabel is already "at costuming" and excited about seeing me there. At costuming? Did she really have to go ahead and say something like that? I think Ma definitely must be hanging around with her daughter a little too much, when it comes to saying those lame-ass drama phrases. I mean, it's bad enough having your sister say that, but once you hear your mother talking like those people, you know she's lost, lost, and too far gone to save. Yet another depressing dip in the roller-coaster ride of my hometown. At costuming, eh? Is that what I'm going to have to listen to today from my ma? I guess the tree doesn't fall far from the apple these days. Hey, I look at it this way—the good thing about going to a play with my ma is that we can sit next to each other, shut the fuck up, and let Shakespeare talk for a few hours. Hours? I don't even know. Shit, when was the last time I've been to a play?

I definitely like Shakespeare, but I'm not—don't get me wrong—some kind of scholar or anything; I've only read a few here and there. The worst mistake ever, and it almost caused me to boycott Shakespeare for good, was that my sixth-grade teacher assigned us *The Tempest.* Sixth grade, I said! I mean, are you kidding? I tried reading that fucker just last year, and I *still* didn't get it. I don't understand what kind of rush people are in to shove Shakespeare down other people's throats, but do you really think a fuckin' eleven, twelve-year old can handle that shit? I remember when that thing was assigned, as a little kid, I tried reading the first page, didn't know what a "boatswain" was, so I threw the book across the room and flicked on a sitcom or something, no problem with my conscience. Hey, the people on the sitcom were talking to me, me, age twelve, at least. Do you know what else really kind of ruined Shakespeare for me? When someone explained to me that people didn't really talk in Elizabethan England in rhyme and verse and poetic images and everything like that. Man, that totally bummed me out. Think about it, why would someone try to write something that doesn't go along with how people really speak? After reading Shakespeare for the first time, I tried to put myself in his position, the way it would have been like four hundred years ago. I envisioned people going up to him backstage and rhyming their congratulations, shit like that, but that's not how it went down at all. They probably talked just as boring as I do, come to think of it, but maybe with fewer curses. Damn—that's another bad habit I got to take care of one of these days. First the harshing on people goes, then the whiskey, and then the curses, okay?

Also, I once did an oral report on the Globe Theater when I was a senior in high school—I did okay, but the bastard docked me half a grade because I used the word "irregardless." Apparently, that's not a word, but it is my teacher's pet peeve—just my luck. Oh, I just remembered the last time I've been to a play—also Shakespeare—it was *Macbeth* and I saw it with this black girl I was dating a few years back. She took me to this theater in Harlem, and they were doing the play set in Harlem in 1990-something. I have to admit the idea was good, but those sorry motherfuckers just could not pull the shit off. Some hip-hop homeboy rapping the dagger speech just ends up being silly. And the worst part of the whole thing was the battle at the end, when everyone had machine guns instead of swords. I got to tell you, those bastards opened fire, and it was like my head was going to split open. Loud as anything you've ever heard, dude—imagine if the people in my apartment building heard that shit? But there was just a thunderstorm of gunplay, and all the older people in that fuckin' theater *scattered,* kid, leavin' in a hurry!

Man, if you think it's a defeat to go back home, you should try going back to your old high school. That is truly the lowest you can sink. Now, you have to understand where I'm coming from with all this; I dreaded the idea of high school for as long as I can remember *before* I went to high school, I hated every period of every day *during* high school, and I look back having graduated high school with nothing but a pure loathing and utter resentment. I have made a specific effort not to speak to a single person, teacher, or school official from high school (besides yesterday with Nicole, I guess) since I graduated from the motherfucker. And judging by my conversation with Nicole in the golf course, let's be honest, do you really think I'll be looking anyone else up? I'm certainly in no hurry to do that—let's try to keep life-altering events to a minimum for the next little while. But I'm sure there are a lot of people I used to know who are probably still all into high school functions; they help with the canned-food drive and everything like that, so I have to be on the lookout. That kind of guy will just be so depressed if this production goes down and people come and go without seeing him there. There's no way I want to run into the valedictorian from my year, whatever the fuck his name was, whatever the fuck his grade-point average was, or the homecoming queen, or anybody like that. I just want to go in, sit down for however long it takes, see Isabel, and once that fuckin' curtain drops, I'm outta there, no need to hang around. And the worst part of that, the reason that plan probably won't work for shit, is that my mom is so big into community functions, and everybody in town knows her, so I'm positive we're going to run into all sorts of people that I don't really need to talk to at this point. Maybe there will even be some people there who heard that my girlfriend killed herself. Wouldn't that be a great ice breaker? Sure, I can picture it: "Oh, I heard about what happened, and I'm really sorry—so tell me, how do you *feel?* Well, enjoy the play!" You think I'm kidding, man, but you don't know the people from my hometown—they'll do shit like that on you if you're not careful. And by the way, if you think I'm going to meet people for the first time and say words like "protagonist" or "denouement," well then you just don't know me too well, and I definitely should have done a better job explaining to you what I'm all about.

So I guess the performance is at noon, or around that time, which means I don't have all day to get ready. I got to steal more of my dad's clothes, and take another shower, which I don't need half as bad as the one I took yesterday. First, though, I finish my bagel, finish the A section. The news inside is nothing but bad: international, local, metro, national—bad news spread all around. The scary thing is, think of it this way, think of this scenario: take someone, like on the subway, who you bump into—accidentally, man—and he gives you a dirty look. You probably, if you're like me, usually look away and pretend you don't notice, right? But maybe there's one of those days when you ain't in the mood, so you look back. And maybe there's one of those days when neither of you are in the mood, and it causes a huge fight. So there's a fight, and if someone happens to have a gun, then the other person is dead. Well, that's exactly what politics is, except on an international scale. Only problem is, when it's on the subway, whatever two fuckheads do doesn't bother my ass, but when you got powerful people fuckin' with the environment and little kids and chemicals and shit, then it becomes a different ball game. So I like to read the paper in the morning, because it puts me in a bad, cautious mood for the rest of the day. I gotta walk around scowling, making sure no one's trying to put a fuckin' knife in my back, making sure no one's gonna take what's mine.

But anyway, after the coffee and the bagel, there's only one thing to do, because you don't want to have to go to the bathroom during a play or anything, especially a bathroom that you used to go to in high school. Nah, I'd rather go in my house—who wouldn't—and I walk up those stairs like they're a splintery plank over shark-infested waters, and into the bathroom. Making sure not to even glance in the mirror this time, I take a deep breath and sit on the toilet. And all that's left to do is wait. With no warning, it all comes out at once, and it's definitely been worse in terms of pain, but there's no question about it, the extraordinary stinging is there, and I can definitely smell the presence of blood in the room. You have no idea how sweet the smell of plain old ordinary shit would be right about now, but the only sense in the room is that salty-ass scent of blood, bad blood. Of course, you can't be sure until you wipe, and I put it off for a minute or two, looking around the room, not wanting to be depressed or anything. And when it's time to wipe, I sneak a peek and—I hate to say I told you so—there's blood smeared all over the tissue. And with the second wipe, there's not that much more blood, which I guess is a slight improvement, but I'm telling you, if this keeps up for a few more weeks, I'm definitely calling a doctor. I mean, this just isn't how it's supposed to happen. But, hey, no real chunks this time, so things can't be all bad. And Clamor starts pawing outside, and I'm thinking maybe he smells something unusual, which I wouldn't be surprised about, or maybe he just can feel something not being right, or maybe it's that I've been in for too long, but he breaks me out of my trance of self-pity. So I hurry up and finish, then I flush the evidence. And that's that! Now, put it out of your mind, and act like you're not scared shitless.

I haven't driven a car in months, so whenever I come back home, it's always cool to motor around town for a little while. I usually like to go out, pop the radio on, and cruise. Only thing, the high school is about a three-minute drive, so I won't get the chance to do anything too crazy, and plus my mom's in the passenger side—took a lot of charm to convince her that I could take the wheel, that I remembered how, that I wouldn't fuckin' wrack the car goin' twenty miles an hour. Trust me, there's only a certain level of coolness you can attain with Ma in the front seat, goin' twenty, and stepping on the brake pedal every other block for some kind of stop sign. But it feels good to be behind the wheel in any case. I can put the priority of coolness on hold for a few minutes, I guess. And with Clamor checking us out from the living room window, I coast down the block, caressing the steering wheel of my folks' station wagon. It might not be cool to you, but there's no better car to cruise in than this thing. It's nice and anonymous. We've had it since forever. And I start to focus on *Romeo and Juliet,* and try to remember things from it, events, some lines, 'cause it's been a while, and I'm in sort of a groove—driving and thinking good, constructive thoughts really do go hand in hand—but Ma pipes up, with another agenda altogether.

"Sweetie, if you don't want to talk about this, I'll understand." Dramatic pause, just like Isabel would do. I don't stop her, I just check the rearview, but there's no activity behind us to busy myself with. This I gotta hear. "But I was reading this article in this magazine—it was very interesting." Great, Ma, send me a copy. Not to be mean, but she shouldn't start things off like that when I'm trying to prepare myself for the play. I mean *Romeo and Juliet* isn't something you should show up to without your guns loaded. You've really got to be ready for what the fuck is going on, or you're going to be lost, bro. "Did you know that more females than males, uh, attempt suicide, but that more men actually die from suicide than women?" Damn. My mom's got balls, man. And Ma's innocent question is the javelin through the helium balloon of my thoughts. Boom! There's total silence as I stop at a four-way, looking around real carefully, because it gives me something to do. Ma now realizes maybe she shouldn't have brought the shit up in the first place—the statistics of suicide—so she does what mothers—all women, in my experience—usually do, which is to make matters worse by trying to make them better, and keep talking, keep talking. "What I mean is, females will use pills and razors, and so forth, but men will usually use guns and, uh, other violent means." God, keep trying to fix it, and you know it'll be broke for good. Again, I don't want to harsh on her too bad, but there was no real reason at that point to bring it up, especially on the way to a play and everything; there's just no reason for it, I'm telling you.

But here I go again, I harsh on 'em when they don't talk about Leonia, and then when they do, I nail 'em even harder. My fault. That's just not fair at all, especially since it's a tough enough situation to start with. But I'm telling you this; I'll ease up a little, I will try, but it's not like we're going to have a forum on it or anything, because that's not going to do anyone any good, and it's certainly not going to give Leonia even one more breath, you know what I'm saying?

And I carefully negotiate a left-hand turn, no problem, and then ease the car back into the straight-away, right near the approach to the school. I keep staring out the windshield, but I ain't gonna let my mom flap around in this conversation like a flag in a hurricane wind, man, she's my mom, for fuck's sake. "Mom? Do you know what that stat means? It means that Leonia didn't want to attempt suicide; it means she wanted to die." And now it's my mom's turn to stare through the windshield, with nothing to say, nothing at all, just a knowing nod. I'm happy saying that because it diffuses the conversation just as we're in the parking lot, and it isn't really rude. I stand by what I said—dying's no feat. "I'd like to see the article, though." Can't hurt to add shit like that, man, tie things up with a little bow, we move on, and there's no problem. Really, I do get a little freaked out when Leonia's name comes up and everything, as an instinct, but she can't become a dirty word. This might be something I have to train myself about, but I don't want people to avoid saying her name. Only thing, though, nobody better say anything mean about her, or anything stupid. And no one can harsh on her, man. That's my job.

Mom and I walk across the parking lot, and it's a trip for me to walk with her. I'm strutting a little, got that little limp going. I'm not even sure why I walk with a slight limp in the first place. I mean, I certainly don't have any kind of injury that I know of, and yet I don't think I make a conscious effort to, so what's the deal? Who remembers anyway? All I know is I've done it for as long as I can remember, and no one comments on it, so they must accept it, too. And my mom walks in these little mincing steps with perfect posture, and we make quite a funny little combination. We're walking next to each other, but not too close; we wouldn't want the other person to mess with our separate strides. And I'm reminded of Clamor, who knows the right way and the wrong way to go on walks, man. He knows what the deal is. Me and him have a rhythm, but not me and Ma. Thing is, what do you expect—how many times during the day do I take my mom out for walks? Zilch, man, and all that means is that we still have a lot of learning to do.

When we get to the guy who's selling tickets, whatever good thoughts I have for the play vanish. I'm not trying to bum you out or anything, but it's all I can do not to drag his ass to the side of the building and work him over a little bit, wipe that little smirk off his goateed face. He's this holier-than-thou drama nut with this fuckin' paisley scarf bunched up around his neck and this corduroy green blazer on, and these weird-ass loafers, and he looks preposterous. Dude, all he has to do is ask, and I'll loan him my wine-red, that's all he needs to be saved. He snaps over at me "seven dollars,

please," and my mom throws out a twenty for both of us.
Seven? What the fuck is going on? I guess you can't see
anything or go anywhere these days without tossing down
dough left and right. Great things, like the opera singer, are
free, but for some reason those are the things you would
have paid any amount of money for in the first place. Price-
less. I'm too busy glaring at this guy to thank Ma for spotting
me the dough. I look at this guy's eyes, man, royal blue,
more indigo than anything else, and the insides are moving
all around like billions of little bubbles. This is what worries
me, because he might dress like a moron, but I bet he's read
a lot of plays, and with those eyes, you have to realize he can
get babes; don't kid yourself. Well, if he's around the theater
a lot, and it looks like he is, I know he probably chats up
Isabel like crazy, and I know he's exactly the kind of guy
that is just corrupting the living shit out of her, one of those
people who cause her to be fake as shit and stupid and lame.
"Do you want a program?" and I mean you got to understand how loud he says that shit. My ear was probably two
inches away from his ass, and he goes ahead and yells the
shit. Projection, it's called, right? Talk so the bastard in the
last row can hear you, right? Hey, no argument; if you're on
stage with a soliloquy, go right ahead, that might be necessary, but not in real life—just talk to be heard, and move the
fuck on. I'm telling you, there's just no need for all that
volume. We're not even at Sapphire's, when you come right
down to it. So I ignore him and walk on—I don't need a
program, I know how to spell my sister's name. But out of
my peripheral I can see Ma grab two.

Now if you think Wood Park has a stupid name, get a
load of this theater. It's called the Stewart Center, named
after this kid who died a few years ago. He actually lived in a

house down the block from me back in the Seventies, and supposedly he was playing football with gum in his mouth, choked on the fuckin' gum, and then died while all these kids were standing around crying, totally freaking out. That led to this whole movement about teaching kids CPR and life-saving techniques, and doing role-playing scenarios. I'm happy all that was before my time, because those programs don't accomplish shit, in my opinion. But this Stewart kid, in addition to football and other sports, he was all big into the drama program because he could supposedly sing, so the name of the theater went from, I think, "High School Gymnasium" to "Stewart Center," although it's not in the center of anything at all that I can tell. Poor bastard, chews on a stick of motherfuckin' Juicy Fruit and then dies from it, only to get a theater named after him. Boy, I bet that rich fucker Wood, if he was still alive, was pissed off that he didn't think of that trick in the first place. Wood would have saved his ass a mil', man.

And the kicker is that when I was in high school I was seeing this girl in the drama department who subsequently dumped me, and she told me that during our school's production of *Macbeth*—and believe it or not she wasn't cast as Lady Macbeth—someone uttered the name of the play backstage, and the Stewart kid's ghost appeared and hexed their show. Drama people will say anything to get attention. Like they can't admit that the show sucked because they're bad actors. I watched a rehearsal once, and the shittiness of it all had nothing to do with ghosts. Kids were fooling around, flirting; not respectful of art at all, not like the opera singer was. But anyone knows gum in the mouth (just like a gun in the mouth) will get you every time; I've known that ever since I was a kid. Stewart is proof that not all old wives' tales are crocks of shit—just, like, most of them. Like girls don't mean it when they try to kill themselves. Sorry, Ma, but that's a big old crock. Let's nip that motherfucker right in the bud, okay?

And my ma and me sit down, and I got to hand it to the drama department, 'cause it seems there's gonna be a totally packed house. We're there a good bit ahead of time, and still, it's not the easiest thing in the world to scavenge two center-section seats next to each other—we're pretty much way the fuck back there. It's a small auditorium, but you like to be up close, or at least I do. Of course, the last time I was up front at an event, my ass got dragged off the stage and my head counted the stairs. Good thing I gave my harmonica away, I guess. And there's sort of a nervous murmuring through the whole hall, and I can tell that everyone is either getting or giving a crash course, an 11th-hour colloquium, on Shakespeare or *Romeo and Juliet,* because I can see people totally concentrating on what their neighbor is saying, which, if you know anything about anything, people never, ever do. How do you sum the shit up, man? You had your whole life to read it, and you're about to watch it, so relax and keep your eyes and mind open, you know what I mean? If anyone asked me I'd say the saddest thing about it is that it's a tragedy, a lot of people die, and there's no villain. Tybalt? Nah, Tybalt ain't a villain, man, he's just a punk. You can meet a guy like that any day of the week. Everyone is equally right and wrong in this thing, more or less, and that's impor-tant to remember. It's just like people fighting on subways.

And I'm talking twenty whole minutes before the play's supposed to start, the lights to the theater dim, even though people are still filing in. That's a little weird, to hustle up the audience at the start of the performance, but I soon realize why they do it. Right after the room darkens, three musicians dressed in Elizabethan garb, all small, pretty girls, one carrying a violin, one carrying a mandolin, and one lugging a cello, come to the side of the stage and sit down on stools that I hadn't seen but must have been there all this time. I wish I had noticed them before everyone else did; it would have clued me in that some people were going to sit there for one reason or another, you know? The details, man. But, I mean, Elizabethan garb! That's right! And I look all over in the blackened crowd for the opera singer, man, 'cause this would have been right the fuck up his alley, with the period piece and everything. No offense to the singer, because I dug his shit, but he's not exactly the type of guy who can just hide in a crowd, so I'm looking everywhere for his long red hair, but I just can't find him for the life of me. That's too bad, because I would probably have went up and talked to him. Hey, maybe he has my old harmonica on him, or something. I don't know, thinking about it, I'm probably better off just leaving things where they are. Why ruin things? Funny thing about great performers like the opera singer, maybe they don't feel comfortable being the audience as much as they do having an audience look at them. I watched this great documentary on photographers, and this one old guy who won a bunch of photography honors said he hasn't posed to have his picture taken in the last fifty years. Nuts, isn't it?

But these three musicians on stage look at each other with adorable concentration, and the cello player nods, and they start playing this hypnotic riff over and over that I can't describe too well except to say that it sounds like a playful conversation between a man and a woman. The man asks a question, when it starts low, and then the woman lovingly responds, a little higher but in the same tone. But it's not an argument at all, you see, it's like a flirtatious, affectionate conversation with a lot of word play and double entendres— the kind of conversation that is just a pleasure to eavesdrop on, and you hope never ends. The mandolin player has hair shorter than me, but messy as shit, which I think is pretty cool. She's looking at everything except her instrument, which is just the way it should be done. Her fingers act like metallic rods, so exact and in this sort of divine flow that can only be interrupted by the player becoming self-conscious about it, which is why she doesn't look at them pressing the strings at all. The cello player kind of weirds me out because she's jerking her head every time she strokes the strings, which means that her hair kind of sails around on her a little bit. But once you get used to it, it's no problem, and she does have the most beautiful mahogany cello which looks like a work of art, like a wonderful chocolate statue, in and of itself. She is looking at both the players—sort of like the way Clamor checks me out on walks sometimes—not that she doesn't trust them, just because she fuckin' likes to look at them, just 'cause it's part of the duty. Now the only person who I can't get a clear read on is the violin player, because she has her eyes clamped shut, as if she's afraid to look at the utter beauty she is creating and the complete rapture that her audience is under. And I swear—I'm not exaggerating— even the people who are just coming into the room, once they sit down, man, they are just watching and shutting up. Something about a song, man, puts you right on the verge of a fond memory and a bilious teardrop; that's the best part of music. What's up, dude? Bilious? You didn't think I knew that word? *Please!* And fuckin' give the drama director a raise, because I was in Nowheresville, New Jersey, a few seconds ago, but a couple bars of this staccato riff, and it truly is Verona, Italy, the seventeenth century, and I'm ready for the ride. I'm under the spell. I look over at Mom, who has a tear in the corner of her eye already, because the music really is so beautiful. For some reason she has her head tilted to the side, the left, probably not even noticing that she's sitting that way. When your head is tilted and you're crying, the tears only flow down one side. My ma, she's under the spell, too. The same one as me, or her own?

With the curtain still closed, this fuckin' *adult,* who I can only guess is the drama director, comes out onto the center of the stage, and the music stops. The crowd breaks into a loud ovation, and I start clapping, too, because the musicians were up there for such a long time and they played so beautifully. And the funniest thing happened; instead of the musicians bowing and accepting the applause, which I completely expected them to do, the director, this guy with a reddish beard and a thinning hairline, starts bowing and beaming, like we clapped because he appeared before us. Shit! I totally misread that, man. Had I known that was the purpose of the applause, you can damn well bet I would have held my peace. I might even have booed the motherfucker, trying to steal the kids' thunder, man. And what the fuck was the prick doing on stage anyway? Isn't he supposed to just be behind the scenes, supervising the shit? Isn't this a high school performance? I look at my mom, who's smiling, and she gently pats the spot where my knee and my thigh converge, as if to say, "check this out," or "it's all right," or something like that. The guy steps forward, and his smile vanishes, as if he just thought of something horrible, or had to get serious, like when they shift from a happy holiday greeting at the top of the newscast to a story about a typhoon in India. And in an even, British-type voice, he speaks the prologue to the play, the part, if you've never read it, where the whole situation is set up, that these two powerful families are feuding, and that Romeo from one family and Juliet from the other fall in love, and they both end up dead. But when he gets to the part about the "two hours' traffic of our stage," I am glad it's him saying that part, and that it's not just some kid trying to get a few credits and a couple chicks by joining the drama club. It's like this guy, by performing the prologue, is admitting that he's apart from the performers, and it all works out. I think it's going to be a great play. *Romeo and Juliet,* man, if you've never read it, you really should—Shakespeare was on to something in a big way. And when that older guy is finished with the short prologue, the applause kicks in again, and this time he just walks away without acknowledging it, because he's in the role deep now, and the three musicians start it up again, with even more spirit, and they're playing that same conversational riff that must have been written by someone who's been to Verona, who was born in Verona, or whose name is Verona, for all I know, and it must have been written in 16 fuckin' 01.

The funny part about this play is that it starts off as a regular street scene, with people milling all about, and there are little kids on stage, who must be the younger relatives of the actors, or something like that. Boy, with all those tots running around, that must have been a real pleasure at rehearsal. You'd need a babysitter, not a director. But in all honesty, it's a great effect, seein' all those kids up there, and they are wearing these clothes from the old school, and seeing all the effort they put into this whole thing makes me feel really bad about griping about the seven; that was kind of uncalled for, especially since it turned out not to be my money. Another good thing about the scene was that, totally out of the blue, they had this little kid walking a dog across the stage, left to right, this little wolf dog. Of course, it had nothing to do with the play, but the audience kind of perked up, trying to get a better look at the dog. I'm sort of glad that Isabel didn't bring Clamor out onto the stage. He's such a ham, he would have gone to each audience member and licked 'em, or demanded some kind of personal love or attention. Would have stole the show, my dog.

For me, the play takes a turn for the worse big time when Romeo comes out on stage, because you expect him to look real dramatic, real romantic and everything, but this guy looks like he's on sabbatical from the fuckin' football team— he's nothing but a sausage in a brown vest and a white poet's shirt, like the kind Morrison used to wear on stage. I mean, not to rail on the bastard, because I admit the guy is pretty handsome, and I'm sure someday if he goes to college, he'll make his fraternity brothers proud and the sorority swans swoon, but he's about as fragile and sympathetic as a fuckin' nuclear bomb. And he has to open up with the line "is the day so young?" which is said when apparently Romeo is so in love with this other girl—not Juliet yet, some other kabob—that he can't keep track of the time and everything. That's the first line, real important, supposed to show how wistful and enamored he is. But he recites the line, and his voice is so damn froggy that it sounds monotone and ridiculous. And no offense to the kid, 'cause he's showin' me that he has a pair, but a Shakespearean loverboy with a Northern New Jersey accent just isn't where it's at at all. I slump down in my chair and pinch the bridge of my nose. This is going to suck. This guy is horrendous because he is trying so desperately to remember his lines that he forgot to act. I know the guy has a lot to remember—it's a big part, I'll give him that, but come on, stud, bring something to the table, will you? Haven't you ever been in love? And here I thought the drama director knew what he was doing. I think I'd prefer sitting in actual traffic for two hours—never mind the traffic of the stage—at least then you won't have sausages there trying to entertain you.

Now, I know how the basic plot of the play goes, and I did, in fact, like the musicians, but I'm truthfully only here to see my sister. And it's a few minutes until she shows up, so I'm drifting a little, thinking about all sorts of things about this play, extraneous things. I'm wondering about the choices I've made in the last day or two, some of the things I've agreed to do. It seems like I've done them for all the wrong reasons, and that there's just no way things like mushrooms or ex-girlfriends are going to bring any kind of peace or resolution to my life. Those things aren't going to turn my shit brown. I mean, here I am sitting through a questionable version of *Romeo and Juliet,* a love story that ends in tragedy—is this exactly what I need at this point? I mean, I'm trying to be a nice guy, but I've got to take care of myself while I still can, if you know what I mean. Well, I can try to do normal things, try to at least act normal, make sure that if I do go down for the count, I won't bring too many other people along with me. I'm sure Isabel is going to be great, but *Romeo and Juliet?* Is this even a good idea, *Romeo and Juliet?* What's the point of seeing *Romeo and Juliet* right now when the "to be or not to be" speech is rotating through the ruins of my mind and ricocheting off all thirteen corners of my heart?

So the three musicians finally come back for this scene that seems like it's a masquerade party, and they do this great up-tempo number, and this guy who's sort of like the court jester gets up there and sings a little ditty, and it's nice, because everyone on stage is dancing around a little bit, and that's when I first see Isabel. She's wearing this crazy Elizabethan dress, but it suits her, and I love it. The thing about the theater, like life, I guess, is that it hits you with so much stimulation you have to react to, and it seems that I've been all over the map with it. It's tiring me out a little, so I'm just going to try to groove to Isabel for a while. And it's then that it dawns on me that the whole play is essentially her trying to hook up with this sausage of a Romeo. I don't know about that, man, it makes me sound ridiculous, but that's not the easiest thing in the world for me to deal with. But everything Isabel says is great, and when she does the "wherefore art thou Romeo" thing, I look around at everybody, and people look genuinely moved, the way I must have looked when those musicians were out there, I'm sure. My mom looks really proud. A lot of people in the audience are really pouring their emotions into this play, man, but I got no more emotions to give; you really have to understand that about me. I'm not totally immersed in the thing like I should be, 'cause I only got so much to invest, but I do think Isabel is doing pretty good, at least it seems that way to me—I'm no expert. All I can think about, as the beautiful music of the English language dances on and in and out of my consciousness, is that I really should be in New York City, alone with me, myself, and I—three people who will let me be selfish for as long as I need.

Well, I'm not going to spend the whole time hating Romeo, but the fact is, I know the play pretty okay, and he has to kiss Isabel and all that, and it's lucky I'm towards the back, or I might call a halt to these whole proceedings, and I might take that cello stick or rod—*bow*—and stick it up his ass if he gets too frisky on her. He should cut the charade and just show up to the next scene in his number 74 football jersey; that'd throw everyone for a loop, wouldn't it? I know it's some kind of neurosis or something, but I just can't seem to separate the play from reality. You can't sit there and tell me that the guy who is playing across from Isabel is not digging kissing her and everything like that. Plus, she's going to be prancing around the stage, and being all cute and everything, she just can't help it, and there's just no way people aren't looking at her. They figure it's okay, it's their right 'cause they paid the bucks. I can't help but care, maybe that's the Italian side of me coming through, with all the jealousy and nonsense overprotectiveness.

And, you know, watching Romeo and Juliet as they first meet, you think that Shakespeare might have been overdoing it a little, maybe exaggerating how they felt about each other, so when it all comes crashing down in the end, it hurts that much more. And yeah, he might have been a little excessive, but when I first was introduced to Leonia, I was long gone, there was no turning back. I was giddy as shit, telling all my friends that this was the one, and that I didn't want to hear anything about anyone else's baby because I had the best, and I was never ever gonna leave her. My friends were tellin' me look before you leap, which I guess people have been telling me my whole life. Why would I go ahead and look? It's not like I have far to go to hit the ground, man. We met at a bar in Hoboken, New Jersey, which must be the college bar capital of the world, pound-for-pound, and I must have found the right bar at the right night, and friends were there, and we met, and we talked, screaming right over the noise all night long. I did this move that night, which I'll let you in on. If you're ever in a bar, and it's really loud and shit, and you want to talk to someone, pretend you have to lean in on her and talk right in her ear. Pretend you just want her to hear you, like that's all that's on your mind. It's excellent, 'cause then you got the hand on the shoulder (opposite shoulder if you're really slick), the breath in her ear, and just more closeness. It works like a charm, at least it did that night. Shit, what am I talking about? You probably knew that trick already. But she told me that night—after a dozen Jell-O shots—that she had never met anyone who was more interesting than me. And she never told me that again, no matter how many Jell-O shots I bought her. God, meeting Leonia— that night—I swear, I haven't thought of that in years.

So with Romeo under the balcony I'm content to let the words coat over me, but I'm totally daydreaming about all my personal stars that have crossed me up in life. Yeah, those stars that act like they're shining for you, but it's a glaze of deceit, not a sacred sheen at all. They're all a waste of breath to wish upon, I'll tell you that. And I can hear the words the actors are saying clearly, but I don't focus on them. Instead, I get a perfect picture, amazingly vivid, of myself in the middle of a darkened street in New York City, and Goldheart and Leonia and Nicole are all above me standing on three adjacent balconies, dressed in flowing white chiffon robes, and their hair is gently moving in the breeze, like it does for models in perfume commercials, and I have to think of something to say—one phrase that will fit all three situations. What can I say to make all three of these women satisfied and happy? I am deeper in the daze, and I keep looking at those three girls, until I realize that Leonia has a gun, and she's pointing it at me. For some reason, I wish I could explain why, this doesn't frighten me at all. I just look over at the incredible vision of Goldheart, and she's rocking a baby slowly, back and forth, with her hair still sailing behind her. And then I see Nicole with a peaceful expression on her face, like she doesn't have a worry in the world. I look at her body a little closer, because it looks a little weird, and the funny thing is that she is clearly pregnant, like five or six months, easy, and the only thing is she's holding a gun, and she's got that thing pointed right at her belly, man, point blank. I flinch like a motherfucker, and open my eyes, and Romeo is fuckin' hollering about something that I can't pick up. Damn! That fucker is screaming like he's calling out signals in the fourth quarter. Maybe that'll get you babes at some sorority party, but that kid has to remember that he is wooing the beautiful Juliet. She's young and precious and needs care. It must have slipped his mind or something. And I look at my ma to see if she noticed that I sort of dozed, but she's busy looking at Isabel, with the proudest expression you've ever seen.

It's not that I'm trying to tell that drama director his job, but it seems to me that there is far too much fuckin' kissing going on in this play. I mean Isabel can barely get a word in edgewise before that sausage starts kissing her, and you know what? Mom doesn't seem to mind at all. And the scary thing is, neither does Izzy, from what I can see. I do, though, I'll tell you that right now. I don't blame my dad for not watching the play—no, it's not like I have anything better to do than watch Isabel get kissed by that bulky guy, right? Jeez, I'm tellin' you. And intermission doesn't come a second too soon, 'cause it's right when they're going to be married in Friar Laurence's cell. And I guess the Friar is supposed to be like a hundred years old in the text, but on stage it's this puny little freshman, so the whole thing is really hard to believe. Not that I know the first thing about casting, but I think the guy who came the closest to being Friar Laurence at least in terms of age is the guy who plays the Prince, who I swear was a fuckin' grade *ahead* of me when I was in high school. That bastard must have gotten held behind like seven times—it's probably because school officials let him do drama when he should have been doing his homework, but that's just my take on it.

And when intermission comes, people start goin' crazy and stampeding toward the bathroom, and like five out of the first six make sure they come up to Ma to tell her what a great job Isabel is doing, and I don't really need that kind of attention—plus talking to my ma's friends makes me feel eleven years old again, when I was just as confused as I am now, except about less-confusing things. Plus, I bet one of them, just to be funny, would bring up the earring thing, and that was a big-time find—that ain't to joke around about. I scout around, the people to my right are gone, so I slip out the side door of the theater into the hallway, and no one's the wiser.

They say intermission will be about fifteen minutes, so maybe I'll take a stroll to the car, flip on the radio, avoid all the other people for a little while. You don't understand, I didn't go to these school functions when I was *in* high school; how do you think I feel goin' to 'em now that I've graduated from the damn place? And I go to exit past the main entrance, and that ticket-taking punk with the scarf is there, and sure enough, he's talking to two fairly attractive women, just like I suspected. Caught in the act! I wonder if they mind that he talks so loud, because he's booming, and they're giggling in harmony. Some guys, man, I don't know how they pull that shit off. But I slip past the ladies, and I'm fixing to get some air, like I said, until that fuckin' voice skids to a stop in the conversation, and all I hear is, "Sir, if you don't retain your ticket stub, please be advised that you will be refused re-entry." What the fuck is this one talking about? Re-entry? What am I now, a fuckin' space shuttle or a human being? Doesn't he know Isabel is Juliet? I'm sorry, he may just be doing his job, but it sounds suspiciously like he's trying to impress some females on my dime.

"I'm just goin' to my car." I stare the bastard right in those crystal blues. Out of my peripheral, I can see those chicks, mouths agape, man, and they're fuckin' horrified, probably a little surprised at my scowl—which I can't help— and my tone. What? Don't they know the secret to good theater is a little conflict? I bet even Aristotle knows that. Listen, first of all, I didn't start it, and second of all, you don't talk to other people like that, man. Someone gives you an administrative position handing out tickets and it goes right to your head? I understand when I attended the school I wasn't allowed to leave whenever I felt like it, but don't tell me what to do four years later, or I'm liable to go fuckin' berserk on your ass. So he closes his eyes dramatically and kind of whisks me away with the back of his hand, as if he's *above* tusslin' with me a little. So before this whole intermission gets wasted arguing with this punk, I wheel around and go out to the parking lot, but I can hear the two chicks giggling mischievously, which I take to mean that they're havin' one on me, which I don't appreciate. But I did kind of like the one on the left, I gotta tell you.

And there's nothing to do out in the parking lot, except watch parents smoking cigarettes. Other than that, I'm alone. No one is bothering me. Off in the distance I can see like eight people jogging around the football field, and they remind me of the planets of the solar system, all orbiting around the hub of the field, all at their own pace, all with separate reasons, I'm sure. I hate jogging, but if I was going to jog, why would I do it on a track around some field instead of on the streets where you can actually see things, where things move around sometimes, where there's some traffic? I don't know, man, I can't think of a defense, except that at a track you're communing with other runners. And I look over and I can see a woman and a man side by side, smoking, except the man has a Walkman on, probably listening to the game or something. Does that depress you as much as it depresses me? Well, it's not hard to be depressed, speaking personally, because aspects of *Romeo and Juliet* are just devastating me right now. I mean, look at it—love and death always go hand in hand. Well, if that's too much for you to take, remember the only difference between death and love—one supposedly lasts forever, the other makes you think of classical music.

And the play resumes—I slide back inside without slipping a dirty look to the guy with the goatee—are you proud of me?—and things in the play just get worse. More people start dying, and Isabel is crying more and more. I never did like watching her cry, not even if she's faking. But the strange thing is, she's doing such a good job up there that I know she means it. She's really drawing off something deep inside herself, just like I've always heard good actors can do. Maybe that hype is actually true. Staging her self-destruction for the whole town to see is no accident. Who in their right mind would want to play Juliet, a girl who just fuckin' collapses for the thrills of the world? And after intermission, the tears flow, and, man, this shit is a cry for help, done with taxpayer funding, in the confines of a drama program. Shit, haven't these people heard of Neil Simon, slapstick, something like that? They name the theater after a tragedy, they perform tragedies on the stage, the classrooms and hallways are filled with the apocalypse, and then they send you out on the streets with an eight-by-ten glossy piece of paper and a robe, and they expect you to be a well-adjusted barrel of laughs? Who's doing the math?

And things really start getting hairy when my sister is up there with that vial of pseudo-poison in her hand that that little kid of a Friar hooked her up with. She's got that small vial dangling limply between her thumb and forefinger. There's this pencil-thin silver spotlight on her, but it's so thin it doesn't even get all of Izzy's face. It's a really cool effect, especially since the people who run lights for these shows are usually just kids from the Audio Visual department; they aren't pro light men or anything. You can sort of see the outline of her face, and most of her mouth—it's pretty eerie. But the main thing is that for some reason you can see every droplet of liquid in that vial, dancing, teasing, tempting, calling. And I'm up there watching Isabel depart from Juliet and act out the suicide. I can see the expression on her face, and it's just the one that I always picture Leonia had as she caressed the trigger before it all came crashing down on the bathroom floor. When I see Isabel acting, it all finally makes sense, it makes sense what an actor does, why good actors do what they do. Isabel may need to act, just like the opera singer needs to sing. It's what they do. What do I do? But Isabel looks alive, *alive,* man, as she wonders about the mystery of the liquid in that vial. And she looks a skillion times more genuine than she ever does at the dining-room table, and she's got a great act going up there, and if I had such a great act, I mean, maybe I wouldn't end it either, not even when I came off the stage. And you gotta see it, man, my kid sister is taking her time, going through the ins and outs of the suicide plan, and I realize that no one in the crowd has moved in a while. Isabel's voice, which always takes up the dinner table, is now taking up the whole auditorium. And when Juliet decides to take the non-lethal poison, the weird substance, Isabel shrieks, "Romeo, Romeo, Romeo!" and the words knife through the hushed room like cones of razor blades, and the echo comes back to my ears: Leonia! Leonia! Leonia! And Isabel drinks every last drop, and then collapses onto the bed.

You're not going to believe what happened, but after she finished that long speech, a couple people in the audience off to the side actually started to clap. I craned my neck and tried to periscope my head to see if I could get a look—just a glimpse—at the type of person who would clap after Isabel went through that. Couldn't tell, though—too dark. The only reason I felt like applauding was that there was a split second in the speech when Isabel kind of stumbled over her lines. Don't get me wrong, 'cause it was totally minor, but I loved it, 'cause it wasn't perfectly flowin', it wasn't like a machine—it was like a human being up there. To get a little reminder, like a private message, that it was still my sister and not Juliet was a really great gift. Nobody else probably even noticed that Izzy slipped a little, but it was a real highlight for me.

I gotta tell you, you're going to think I'm kind of stupid, probably, but when you think about *Romeo and Juliet,* you don't really remember right away that two people kill themselves at the end of the thing. At least I don't. I mean, I think of romance and love and swordfights in Italian *piazze,* but you don't think of how it all comes crashing down. Isn't that so? And I mean, me—if it would have occurred to anyone, don't you think I would have been more sensitive to it than your average guy? But I had to grip the side of my seat when Romeo went fuckin' nuts and ended up poisoning himself, and then Isabel goes and plunges that dagger into her stomach. Yeah, that was a real pleasure, watching Isabel keel over and die, as the whole fuckin' town looked on, seven dollars lighter, all of them, munchin' popcorn, if they had any.

And the thing about the audience in the high school is that when the Prince says at the end that there never was a story "of more woe than this of Juliet and her Romeo," you can tell straight off that everyone takes him at his word. Oh, yeah? You think *Romeo and Juliet* is sadder than all this shit I been through? Damn, man, I could tell you some stories. Gotta say, I felt like hopping up on stage, slipping on a tunic, and upping the ante on the kid, going straight ahead and letting everyone hear a real bad story, and a real real one, besides, believe it or not. I wish I knew why everything about Leonia is like a giant black hole in the galaxy of my mind. But there's still a part of me that wants to tell everyone I see about what happened—is that bad? See, that's the thing—it's practically all I'm thinking about, it's all I want to talk about, but for the most part I can't get word one out. Not that that makes any sense or anything.

And when the play and the dying and the applause are over, Mom springs up and gets ready to dart backstage to hang out with the actors, which could perhaps be the last place on the planet that I need to be. So I toss my mom the keys to the car, and I'm walkin' home. She's okay with that—I'd probably be cramping her style. Good fuckin' play, and Romeo even got a little more bearable as the play went on—again, I'm really sorry I harshed on him a little bit.

Walkin' home, goin' the same route I took all through high school could be the best thing ever for me. Romeo, Juliet, and Isabel are just kicking around in my brain, and I mean, you gotta know that I'm one of those people that think there's gotta be some significance, and there's gotta be some message, something I can learn about this whole mess. What's the use struggling through that play if I can't work it to my advantage? And I know right off the bat the eternal question—why when you think of Romeo and Juliet do you think of their amazing love and not their death? Why when you think of Romeo do you think of him as the golden-tongued romantic instead of just another sausage who killed himself? And why when you think of Juliet do you think of the embattled child, born to love, rather than someone who plunges a knife into herself? You know what I mean? So why should my Leonia be any different? Why do I always have to associate that woman with that bullet? Why can't I remember the bar in Hoboken? And the love in her heart— that once I got to it I snuffed it, kid, I really did—why can't I remember the original love? And as I see twin black terriers being led down the block towards me, I do, in fact, think of the *living* Leonia, of the way she would have busted off, mid-sentence, no matter what I was saying, and sprinted across the street to give each of them a kiss. Just like Clamor. Leonia comes through for me when I need her most, gives me a memory that I actually smile about.

And smiling, I think of what it would be like to walk home after spending this exact same day with Leonia, my old girlfriend. I think of some of her inevitable comments to the ticket-taker, how she would have made some peace but still supported me. Some girls I've met, man, they just get you to wondering whose side they're on. But I think of how she would have smothered my resentment of Romeo the first time it reared its unnecessary head. And I can picture Leonia in the backseat, rolling her eyes when my ma talked about this bizarre theory of suicide, that most girls are just sending a message and don't really want to do it. Fuck that, man, that gets disproven day after day—even in *Romeo and Juliet,* for Christ's sake—and Leonia would have known that. Anyone with any common sense at all would have to agree with me on one point—Juliet wanted to die, wanted to, man, she wasn't just bluffing. Nah, trust me, if Shakespeare had ever heard that there was such a thing as a gun, that girl would have went ba-boom, kid!

VI

RED LIPSTICK ON THE RIM
OF A STYROFOAM CUP

So I'm sitting at my kitchen table in 4D, back in the big city, flipping through the A section of *The New York Times* from the day before. Couple of 'em were stacked up when I got back. Dude, you can't expect me to remember stuff like suspending delivery at a time like this. Especially since those punks didn't publish an obituary or a story or anything like that, not that I saw. I guess a lot of people die all the time. I'm flippin' through, scanning past international shit, but really trying to zone in on some of the national, and also evaluating in the background of my mind how it all went down, how the weekend in my hometown finished up. Living is an excuse to reminisce. Of course, reminiscing by yourself is a little pathetic, but my partner's gone, so what can I do?

After I got home from the play, I slipped on the clothes I was wearing two nights before, when I came from the city originally, threw the shit I was wearing down the clothes chute, so Ma won't send me on a one-way guilt trip next time we talk, and man, I was out the door and bounding down the block, not looking forward to *anyone* seeing my ass on the way out. I could have waited until my dad came home, to bond with him in our own way, and maybe get a ride back, but why bother? Seems like I already accumulated enough baggage for me to just mark it down as a weekend, done and over, and let's move on, you know? I know Izzy would have wanted to hear my rave review for her show, but what am I going to do, tell my little sister she's a good kisser or something? What kind of bullshit is that? And Ma would have loved me to stay over for dinner or whatnot, leftover split-pea, but I didn't think the whole atmosphere would be any different than the last time, so I just jet, man—think long, think wrong; just fly. I didn't even say "see you" to my brother Clamor, but don't think less of me or anything 'cause of that. It's not like we're any kind of lame teenage chicks or anything, where we have rules or formalities or that kind of stuff. I mean, you just gotta know that we don't have that kind of relationship. Clamor's thinking on the matter is much like mine—if you think you gotta go, well then what are you waiting for, motherfucker? Now, you'll hear me bitch from time to time about a wide variety of topics, but you'll never hear me get uptight about that kind of procedural stuff, man; my attitude is that people should just do what they gotta do, and not worry all that much about being called inconsiderate. Anyway, I don't generally want to consider people who call me inconsiderate, you know? They just don't get it, and they certainly don't get me. Last thing I'll say on that, and I don't mean to harsh, like I said, but if you need my help, you probably don't deserve it.

Now, having said all that, and maybe I went a little too far back then, I did leave a note on the dining-room table. Man, I know you're going to want to know exactly what I wrote, word for fuckin' word, but I can't give you that information right now. I mean, I'm sorry, but my mom's pad doesn't come in carbon copy, so I can't even produce a duplicate for the public record. More or less, from memory, I think I wrote thanks for having me, I feel good, and I'm ready to head back to the city and go back to school. I think I said good job, Iz', just to cover my ass, and then I said take care of Clamor, and to give him a treat for me. I put a little doodle on the left, just like old times. Then I signed it, and my p.s. was—"see you soon! And NYC, clear the women and children off the streets!" Now you know why I did that, right? My ma is the ultimate worrier, so I gotta write little things like that to show her that I still got some spunk in me, and that I really ain't going anywhere. I know just what to say to make Ma feel all right; that's why I never know why she has no idea what I need to hear—isn't that crazy? But I try to leave everybody with a vibe of positivity. You won't believe this, but they probably need a pep talk as much or more than I do, so if I can help them out a little, especially if it only takes a second, then I'm going to do it for 'em.

But as far as I'm concerned, I gotta now go toe-to-toe with New York City, and I don't think any championship boxer goes into a fight thinkin' he's gonna lose, so that's why I had to talk a little trash. I mean I don't think I talked trash all weekend—that's what family'll do to you—so I summoned up my old character, and I was out the door. Hey, worse comes to worst, maybe someone will get a laugh out of it. And the tough part of it is that as I was writing the note, I'm thinking—a note. Jesus, Leonia, a note. Is that so hard, to scribble a note? Can't you see how I might need a note? Shit, I wouldn't have showed anybody. But then reality rides into town, and hey, what am I, a fuckin' moron? What could the note say that her deeds didn't, right? What kind of idiot would see her dead on the floor, parts of her all over the fuckin' joint, and then still be searching for a note. Hmm, what do you think she means? Like there are so many ways you can interpret her actions, right? Listen to me, man, sometimes I bother myself.

The one thing that happened back in Jersey before I left that I should tell you about was like the biggest bummer in history. This one, man, you could put right under the heading of "just my luck." I don't know if it was the walk or the play or what, but son, when I got up to my room I crashed like a fucker. I went inside the house, took Clamor, and we went up to bed and *crashed,* Timberlands, jeans, everything still on, I'm telling you. And have you ever had like multiple dreams in one? Well I think I had three or four, and they were all about Michelle, for God's sake. Who knows why—I certainly don't. So I slept funny, all contorted and everything, because Clamor, sleepin' diagonal, only left me a sliver of the bed—the part with all the wood and shit, just like Leonia used to—and I woke up with my back in knots and my head all staticcy, if that's a word. But the thing that made me most sad of all was that I could feel my left ear lobe stinging like a motherfucker, and my heart was beating up there, which was awfully strange, you know? And so my instinct is to touch it, but I know that it'll just hurt more, so I don't, but I do go downstairs, cursing a little bit. Every step and a new part of me creaks; it feels like I'm a hundred years old, and I can't think of anything about me that feels healthy. So I walk down kind of gingerly, and Clamor's on my heels, 'cause it's not like he's gonna stay if I ain't there, right? I can hear each of my steps echoed in quadruple as we go down the stairs, and I don't even check to see where my boy is, 'cause I know we have a system; he won't trip my ass up. He did once, but it was late, and he was tired, or maybe I fucked up—who knows?

So I go into the bathroom and check my ear and it's like crimson red, man, closer to maroon, with rivers of veins all over the place. Shit, and the shitty part of the whole thing is that there's this milky pus kind of seeping out of the hole that the earring made. Looks like Ma was right and I guess it did get infected after all. I thought Nicole said she knew what the fuck she was doing, man. But it's looking really bad right now, and before I take it out, 'cause I can't even bring myself to touch my own ear, I just lower my head into my chest, close my eyes and start shakin' my head, depressed as all hell. Now I hope you realize I wasn't upset 'cause my earlobe might have been fucked up, or 'cause the earring thing didn't necessarily work out. I mean, who gives a shit about stuff like that? That's like a temporary setback or something, and man, I've had enough permanent setbacks to shake off the temporary ones okay. No, what really got me was that it seems that every fuckin' decision I've made on my own in recent memory has come back to bite me on the ass, they just want to haunt my ass forever. Every damn decision. I ain't exaggerating—I was the one who took it upon myself to beg Nicole to sleep with me; I wish I could tell you how many times I asked her, until I knew she was going to just break down, you know? I can be persistent like a little kid if I really want something, especially back in high school. Who do you think suggested that me and Leonia should move in together? And jumpin' on stage at Terra Blues, sure, that was a little bit of the whiskey's fault, but it really boiled down to being my decision. It all just seems to backfire, man. I mean, a million guys get earrings, don't they? But only mine gets infected—it just doesn't make sense to me. I can't wait for something to go right, whether it's something as stupid as an infected earlobe, or something as serious as Leonia scattered all over the bathroom (and a little of the kitchen, like I said) floor. And speaking of all that, who am I to say that the lobe is stupid and Leonia is serious? Maybe certain people can get a chuckle out of either, right? But now I'm feeling sorry for myself, which I told you to call me on if I ever did. So I pluck that fuckin' thing out of my ear, and it's depressing, 'cause I thought it was some kind of mystical signal, and maybe it was, or maybe it was just saying that I'm not the type of guy that should wear earrings—again, I don't know; no one tells me anything. And the hole in my ear looks pretty bad, like there're all kinds of rips and torn skin and veins where they ain't supposed to be. That sucks, but it'll heal. Let's keep this in perspective—I mean, Leonia's wound won't heal. You know what else I heard somewhere? That the damage that American troops did during the Gulf War did things to the planet that will never heal. Think about that: *never*. Well, that's what Leonia did to herself. And I guess I inflicted some wounds on her that never ended up healing, if you want to look at it that way. I slip the earring into my pocket, 'cause if I throw it away, Clamor might get to it, being curious and all, and he doesn't need to start eatin' diamonds; he gets enough fuckin' minerals. Earring operation: failure (surprise, surprise).

So that got my ass out of the house real quick, 'cause I needed air and space. Air, space, what's the difference? Who gives a shit, kid? I hear Washington D.C. has a museum totally devoted to those two topics—maybe that's where I should hang out. Do you think there are any women there? Doubt it. So I wait for the bus, and I pull out this book that I clipped from Isabel's bookshelf right before I left. It's called *The Remains of the Day,* by some guy. I heard it was a pretty good movie, plus it says on the cover that it won a couple awards, and I mean, I'm just reading the first few pages, but this fuckin' punk has his shit together, man. The guy telling the story is like some kind of big shot butler in England after World War I, I guess, and man, I gotta tell you, this book is making me hope the bus won't ever come, 'cause I'm psyched enough just hanging out reading this fucker outside as the winds whip up. I mean, you don't really know me one hundred percent, but I think you can guess that I like other types of books besides butler shit, you know? I mean, hand me *Paris Trout* or *Six Out Seven* or *The Goalie's Anxiety at the Penalty Kick* and I'm happy, you know, shit that's a little guttier than this fancy kind of writing. I mean, I guess I've cursed more in the last ten seconds than this guy's done in like twenty pages—he's a butler, remember? I wonder if this guy curses at all, on any of the two or three hundred pages in this book—I doubt it, man. But let's face it, I'm really kidding myself if I think stubble on the chin or curses in my sentences are any kind of indication as to who's raw or who's on the edge, or who can kick your ass after a few whiskeys in a bar. Do you know what I mean? Just like you might not have thought that I like to read. Want to hear something funny? A few years ago, my best friend loaned me *Zen and the Art of Motorcycle Maintenance.* Want to hear something even funnier? I didn't consider him my best friend until *after* he loaned me the motherfucker!

But of course, right when you wish the bus won't come, well nine seconds later the bastard comes screaming and farting around the corner. I actually contemplated hanging on until the next bus, except that this bus stop is along Mom and Isabel's route home from the high school, so I mean, I'm really just a sitting duck, and not a very smart one at that. So I slip into the thing and throw the lady a couple bucks, and she closes those iron doors, trapping you in for the ride whether you like it or not, like a Rahway State Prison on wheels. As I give the lady the money she hammers some buttons, man, and the ticket dispenser vomits my proof of purchase, but I don't take. Man, I've been on too many buses to start keeping souvenirs, or doing things the way I gotta do 'em, procedure, according to some kind of sign. Does that sound stupid? Maybe, man. Go ahead and say so if it does.

I sit down way in the back, next to a window, and I've got the book to get back into; it's a short book; I should be able to break clear ground on it. I think I'm in one of maybe only two seats left that doesn't force me to have a travel partner for the duration. So I'm all alone getting back into it, and I am loving this butler, getting a thrill out of each syllable. It's funny, 'cause the words are glowing on the page, and as I read, I swear I can see the anonymous neighborhoods cruise by in my peripheral. That's kind of funny, 'cause the whole thing I'm reading is supposed to be in the south of England, but it ends up being in the north of Jersey. However, I don't think there are too many butlers, and I'm quite sure that there are no lords or gentlemen around here.

Just when all these things are happening in my book and I put my own life's problems on pause for a second, believe it or not, the bus stops again, and—surprise, surprise—this twenty-something lady sits down next to me, and she's hauling this little baby girl with her. Also, behind her is this world-class sausage carrying all kinds of baby paraphernalia and shit, lugging heavy bags. It's been my experience that the only tangible way that husbands actually help wives is by carrying shit. In my mind, I'm about to get up so they can sit next to each other, but I don't end up moving. I do glance up, and the ma gives me this sheepish-ass smile, like, "I'm sorry I'm gonna have to sit next to you and ruin your trip, but, you know . . ." and she squats down next to me, man, over that seam in the seat that bus companies put to make sure no one gets too territorial or anything. Clearly over, *clearly*. But I don't give a fuck, hey, I ain't fat or anything; I'm slender enough to scrunch a little. The whole thing, though, is a question of comfort. This sucks, I don't care who the fuck is next to me. And it pisses me off a little bit, because now I'm out of the flow of my book, and this particular book is very much about flow and rhythm and timing and everything else that makes me wish I was the only person on the vehicle, except for maybe the lady bus driver. Yeah, I'm way out of the flow of the book and I'm into some kind of alien flow, but of course it's my own thoughts bringing me down and fucking me up, as usual, it seems, at least lately. Jesus, man, why did I have to pick this exact seat? Didn't I tell you that every decision I make on my own comes out snake eyes?

So I'm staring out the window, but it's no kind of transcendent experience like on the bus out to Jersey. And, I gotta say, there are a lot of reasons why. Then it was the night time, and the glass became a mirror and the mirror became some kind of thought provoking monster, plucking specific fears out to the forefront, all the while with the lights of the universe glimmering in the background. The thought that occurs to me most of all is that I had absolutely no purpose to go home. I mean, there was just no reason to do so, was there? What was I thinking? Did I think that this killing would cause my family to think anything different about me, that their behavior would change? Yeah, the thought must have cropped up in my head that Isabel and Ma and Dad would suddenly turn into some kind of sit-com family and we'd have sit-com conversations with sit-com solutions at the end, and only thirty minutes of your time used up. You think that was my goal? You know, I like to think I'm a pretty smart guy, I mean, I know which way is up and everything, but man, I would trade a few of those meaningless IQ points just so my wicked delusions of adequacy wouldn't get me into shitty situations and mindsets like this. It's bad enough what happened happened, right? The last thing I need to do is set people up, like my folks and Nicole and everyone in my hometown, to some extent, to take the fall with me, in a way. Now, this bus window is totally different because it's dirty as shit, just grime speckled all over it, so you don't even want to look at it at all. Trust me, it'll just make you sick. And the bus rides on. It's not the best feeling to be moving, to be in any kind of vehicle, or even walking, not knowing whether you are going towards home, away from it, or in a bad direction altogether. That's not the best feeling at all. Ever been there?

Now, I think the average human body, or certainly mine, is created to take up fifty-three percent of a bus seat. It's just more comfortable when you've got a sliver of your ass on the other guy's seat, that's all there is to it, as far as I'm concerned. But when the chick and her little punk come along and—*occupato*—that's a totally different story. So I finally break down and look over at the two of 'em, after I'm through my initial mood of being all pissy. I don't care who you are, you're telling me a lot about yourself if you can sit right there and just flat out ignore a baby.

Now I'm not trying to say that I would line up to have some drooling little bastard all next to me making noise on a bus, but what a perfect little kid this baby is! This kid has no teeth, and is making these faces where I think she's straining to make some kind of connection. It's like she has all these words and ideas and thoughts in her, and it's all she can do to stay alive without someone knowing what she's talking about. I been there, especially when I was on mushrooms. What a struggle! I hope that kid learns soon that there's no use struggling and putting up that kind of fight. Quit while you're only a little behind. The thing is, the English alphabet only has twenty-six letters. Twenty-six? That is so inadequate, especially for the people with all those thoughts ricocheting around inside of them. Me, I need the twenty-seventh letter to help me speak better. Yeah, that'll get my message across; then you'll know where I'm coming from. Trust me, in my experience, the only people who are not understood are those people who have important shit to say, who are worth understanding. It's funny in a sort of an evil way, the way the world works, isn't it?

But this woman with short blonde hair, real athletic looking, squirms in her seat, rubbing against me, and the two of us watch her little baby clawing like an animal, on her back, feet flying all over the place. That kid busts into a smile like she knows something we don't, which of course, couldn't be truer. Then, the mother starts all this nonsense baby-talk, which to me is the worst thing a mother can do to a kid. I wanted to boot the mother out, put the damn kid on my own lap and read her *The Remains of the Day,* 'cause trust me, she would have at least gotten something out of that, man. Remember, this is like a perfect little baby, right, nothing wrong with her whatsoever—healthy and all, talkin' clean slate—only thing fucked up about the kid is that they got her trapped in this pink pajama bullshit outfit, which I'm sure looks cute to some small sector of our society, but to me it looks like they dressed her up to be some sideshow freak. I mean, is that what we do in America? When someone has a little girl, we fuckin' run out to the most expensive store and buy a pink outfit? But if it's a boy, gotta buy blue, right? Please, man, that's such a load of shit. I'm not saying put a football helmet on her or anything, but for God's sake, give her a chance! Don't go ahead and make her a man or anything, trust me, that's the last thing I want anyone to do, but do you really have to go ahead and dress her up like that? It sucks to me, 'cause there's a great person in there somewhere (you could tell by the struggle), but she's in this devilish camouflage of stupidity, a total lack of dignity and importance, with that flowery stupidity, all pink and cheery, for no good reason. Man, I'm stuck wondering if wine-red workshirts come in small sizes, really small sizes, 'cause, no shit, I'd spring.

I don't care who you are, whenever you spend any time whatsoever with a baby, you got to inevitably think of your own existence, who you are in relation to this thing. Seeing something so small and young can make you feel old in a hurry. And I'm only twenty-one. The thing that has always sort of alarmed me about seeing babies is that my whole childhood is almost entirely a vacuum. What I mean is that the only real sense I can get of myself as a kid is through stories and pictures, and who knows how true those things are? I know they happened; they must have, but what I mean is that in the hallway in my folks' house there are a whole mess of pictures of the four of us. Most of them, though, are of me and Isabel as little kids. Oh, there may be a couple recent ones, like maybe a graduation picture of me or something, or I think one of my sister in a play, but I'm telling you, the last decade is undocumented, unless you count this story I'm telling you, which you probably shouldn't. Anyway, it ain't that hard to tell why Ma hasn't put up family pictures in the last few years—pretty basically, things have really gone downhill. I mean, there you go, there's a picture right up there of me at like *pi* weeks old, like the first bit of my existence, and I'm in Dad's lap, and he's smiling like he was just given a secret treasure from highest heaven, like he's the luckiest guy in the universe. How long did that last, is what I've always wondered. No, really, that's a great question. I mean, look at the ecstasy—it could have lasted a couple years, or maybe even Dad's expression died down the femtosecond after the picture was snapped. Sure—of course Pops can pretend to be happy for a fraction of a second, right? He's only human. That's all it takes for a picture to give you a permanent impression of what a moment was like. But remember, it's only a moment. A picture is an illusion, an encapsulation of coincidence, sometimes. Was Pop pretending? Maybe that's where Izzy gets her inclination to act. But I mean, you take memories like me on Dad's lap and compare them to things recently, and you just got to ask yourself: what's Ma in her right mind going to do, take a picture of him yelling at me or something? Or maybe the time he threw me up against the wall and that picture frame fell on the floor? With Ma screaming and everything? Like that's a cuter conversation piece? Nah, it's just a little more accurate. I mean, in the quest for the truth, the secret is to find all sides. Only thing, sometimes the truth is like a circle: no sides at all.

A really cool picture, I got to admit, black and white, is of me and Isabel kissing on the lips when she was maybe three. That one was funny, down by Long Branch on the Jersey Shore; we used to go there just about every summer. Man, that picture, the expression on my face, it just makes me laugh from the belly every time I see it—when no one's around, at least. When I went home this past weekend, I checked out the whole gallery of pics, and a couple of new ones have actually gone up in the past year or so. You know what the kicker is? Most of them are like my ma and my dad and there's even one of Clamor. Why do you think that is? People putting up photo collages have the same type of evil power that editors for news broadcasts have—trillions of things happen every day, but they get to choose the half-hour that you see. And with Ma, those pictures she has up did happen, sure, but if it was up to me, I would lobby (if I had the energy) for something a little more *representative,* if you know what I'm driving at.

So thoughts are coming ruptured and confusing, if you haven't noticed, because of the baby and the sausage and the horrible reading atmosphere and all the dirt on the window and the cramped surroundings. So, what the fuck, only cowards don't confront whatever is pissing them off, and I look over with kind of this pained expression that I'm really hoping no one can see, and I glance over to the baby on my right, and I got to say that little kid just has the sweetest smile, and those gray fuckin' eyes, and she's looking right at me. It's the weirdest thing, because the really good babies, like really good dogs, can sense when you're in a bad mood, and somehow, without saying a word—but with just a look—can pull you right out of it. Never ever in this world have I met a woman who can do that, man, so if you've got one, hang the fuck on. And before I can help it, my phony-ass smile turns as real as it's been in a while—shit, as real as I think I'll be *capable* of for a while—and I look over at the woman. And all of a sudden I hear my voice croak out, "What's 'er name?"

Now, the woman looks startled, and I don't really blame her, because she must have pegged me for a non-talker straight off the bat, and then all of a sudden I turn into some kind of happy-go-lucky guy. What can I say? Maybe that's manic depression, or maybe just the mark of a good baby. And the saddest part of this whole exchange, something I'm sure I'll never forget, is that the woman looks at me and she says, "Who, me? Or her?" And she points her thumb at her baby. I bet I'll always be able to see that in my head in slow motion, over and over, her asking, "Who, me? Or her?" And, I mean, good God, what is she thinking, that I actually give the first fuck on this sorry planet what her name is? I mean, I wish I knew how people had that in them, to think they're more important than their little kids, or even just as important as their little kids. Man, I'd love to drag her ass somewhere private, away from her sausage, and really explain all the ins and outs, all the implications of her questions, but it sounds like she'll never learn. And I must have looked kind of pissed, because she lets out this embarrassed chuckle and actually hits her forehead with her palm, and then says, "Oh, her!" She shakes her head and rolls her eyes at herself, sort of an admission that she fucked up so bad. Gee, I had spoken clearly, right? What's up with this one? So she says, "Her name is Donna—that means *'woman.'*" And this lady is just bumming the shit out of me. Who gives a rat's ass what the fuck the baby's name *means?* First of all, I speak Italian—I think I know what the word means. And second of all, isn't it important enough that it's the child's name? Isn't that enough on its own, for Christ's sake? Wow, it means woman. Pretty deep. So it means woman—so? I wonder if her husband thought up that little word game. Yeah, I can almost guarantee it.

"Pretty name," I say. See, I'm just as big a hypocrite as the rest of 'em. To me, you see, names are really important. I totally gotta disagree with Juliet on this one. I mean, it's weird, 'cause you can go so many ways with it, like the way a cowboy brands the ranch's name on the asses of his cattle. It's all about ownership, you know. Here on the bus, I'm just looking at the baby, and then looking at the parents, seeing like six or seven mistakes they're making right off the bat.

All that stuff makes me think real hard about Leonia. Now *there* was a name, kid! But don't go blaming the parents for her outcome, man; I know for sure that falls right on me. She was fine before she met me, and everyone knows it. Trust me, everyone knows it. But the thing is, this little Donna ain't gonna be fine at all. Donna. Looking at her also makes me think of this thing my dad once told me when I asked him to tell me the most important job a father has. And we were raking leaves in the backyard and it seemed like he was gettin' all the fuckin' leaves in one swipe, 'cause he was my pop an' he was superman, and he knew just where to swipe the fucker, you know? And all the while, I'm sitting there with my junior rake, the little plastic one my dad got me, and I'm getting like a couple twigs and just a few leaves. Every stroke reminded me how much better my dad was than me.

And while I'm remembering all this, I'm staring at the

little kid, and it seems like the lady is waiting for me to say something, so I sort of continue the story that was going on in my head, except out loud, and I go ahead and say, "I once asked my dad what the biggest job he had as a father was, and he said, *'Devi dare un nome al bambino quando é nato.'* That means: 'you gotta name the baby when it's born.' He's Italian, y'see." And just like I was amazed at her when she didn't know I was asking the baby's name and not hers— and I think I had every reason to be—now it's her turn to look at me like a deer in headlights, like Quayle in that vice-presidential debate I saw a few years back. So I go on. "That always struck me as a real fuckin' shitty thing to tell a kid, even if he was just kidding around. I mean, he got me to thinkin' that a name was such a big deal—it messed me up a little." Now remember that I always said that even some-times when I acted like I was out of control, I was really in control? Well not this time, man, 'cause the memories were coming painful, and the words were spilling out, slaves to inertia. Dude, if you're ever around me and I just start yap-pin' like that, I think you should just let me run out of words, which I'll do soon enough. But the saddest thing of all was that the lady shifted in her seat, totally not comfort-able, and then she looks down at the baby and kind of tight-ens her grip, and then sort of sneaks a peak over at her husband. Man, it sure looks like she can't wait to get to New York City, I'm telling you. I can't wait either, but for totally different reasons, I'm sure. Jesus, I never asked her to sit next to me with that little kid. Trust me, I would have been perfectly content reading my book, letting visions of New Jersey jet by in my peripheral. She sat next to me, you saw it. All these years, I still can't figure out why Dad told me that, though.

And just then, her husband leans over the aisle and says kind of sharply, "Uh, honey, we had that thing we had to talk about." Pretty clever line, buddy. He reaches out his hands, and she slips the baby over to him, and then she shifts around so I can only see her back, and the back of her head. Plus no baby anymore. Don't even ask me how I did that, but I basically frightened the two of them off. Did I curse? Yeah, I think I did curse, come to think of it. God, don't tell me that's what frightened them off. Maybe that's why they're all bent out of shape. I mean, it's not like a kid's gonna understand what word is a curse and what isn't, I don't think. If anything, it's a lot more dangerous to bring the kid up with baby-talk than with the language of the streets. The kid's smart enough to understand that I'm speaking earnestly and passionately, and that I ain't pandering. I bet she never gets any of that at home. I think it sucks that the baby has to listen to her mother translate her name for strangers, if you ask me. Oh yeah, bitch? What's your husband's name, *Salsiccia?*

Well, I ain't in the mood to stare at the smokestacks' exhalations and the malls flanking the turnpike. No need to revisit that shit, 'cause I think I must have worked at every one of those damn places, man. I had so many horrible jobs, man, way worse than the paper route. Maybe it's a good thing the window is dirty—that way I don't have to battle these unwelcome random reminiscences. And scoping out people across the aisle, but totally watching mother and child in my peripheral, I sense that big ol' moron is staring at me hard, like I'm actually going to make a move on his wife or kid or something. I turn myself away from everybody, and force myself now to study the waves and ovals of my fingerprints, wondering why human beings are created the way they are, feeling sick, ready to cry, thinkin' if I get one more dirty look from anyone—anyone—I'm going to go insane, or even more insane. I'm about to pass that fucker a note, and tell him to be careful who he tries to stare down, because the next guy he comes across just might have an ex-girlfriend's gun between a certain wine-red and an old pair of Levis. I mean, keep your fuckin' bad thoughts to yourself, dude, I've got enough of my own. Plus, like I'm really gonna scam on some chick with a baby and a husband? Sure, I've been known to talk to girls on occasion, but I like to think I'm a little more selective than that, for Christ's sake. I mean, big guy, give me some credit. Then I look down to the kid. Damn. That little thing is just mired in that pink outfit. I wonder who thought up the idea that girls are supposed to wear pink, the mother or the father. I bet the sausage was responsible for that one also.

Anyway, like I had a lot to look forward to goin' back to the apartment? Yeah, right, but I was fuckin' psyched when the bus ride was over, 'cause who knows if I would have got into a fight, or ruined the little kid, or whatever. Me on this planet is like a bull in a motherfuckin' china shop, dude, everywhere I look or turn things start tumbling and breaking, and it's just a bad scene all the way around. So I think I might be best just shackled up with invisible chains in my apartment, 4D, but what, is it really like hibernating there until spring is going to renew me (with my rent doubled now that I'm springing for Leonia)?

So, as I know you know, the bus leaves you off at the Port Authority, at Forty-second and Eighth, and, uh-oh, there are a lot more decisions to make. I can take the shuttle and then the 6; I can take the crosstown and then an uptown bus, or just walk. Seems like I've been walking more in the last few days than I ever have in my life. I guess that's what happens when you're in no particular hurry to get places, you know? But I get a token for myself—a buck fifty now, kid, fuckin' rip city—and I just sort of mechanically, like on autopilot, slither down the stairs and slide onto the C train downtown, the local. The subway is pretty funny, because sometimes that thing'll come around the bend roaring, like the noise of the apocalypse, and some other times, like this time, it kind of tiptoes. I figure I'll go down to West Fourth and see what the Village is like. Can't hurt. Ah, who am I kidding? Yeah, all this time I've been trying to be as nonchalant with you as possible, but I hope it didn't slip by you that I'm really just interested in stopping by Michelle's house, if I can even find it. I got to tell you man, words can't fuckin' describe how lonely I am right now. 4D would be like headquarters for the broken-hearted, so I'd rather go to the headquarters of the golden-hearted. Like I think I said before, I don't want to be considered a stalker or some kind of nutcase, but hey, we had a nice enough time, and if it's humanly possible, somehow I've thought of her in some fashion every second since I left her house. Figure worst-case scenario and she hasn't thought of me half as much, but she'd still be willing to do some more shit with me, or maybe at the very least she'd let me buy her some Chinese or something—I don't care, whatever she wants, she made me feel so good and so wanted. I wonder if she likes me sober. The big problem, though, is it's too early to drop by Sapphire's, in case that's her regular place (and plus, it's Sunday, *no one* is there on a Sunday—is it even open?). Not only that, I can hardly re-member the apartment building she took me to, although maybe if I was there—you may recall I had had a few drinks of whiskey.

God, I can't even stand to say the word "drinks" or "whiskey"—it makes my whole damn insides clench up like a fist. There's just no reason to do that to yourself. Man, maybe some Rolling Rocks from time to time, if I'm with a lady or something, but there's no way I'm buying a JD bottle like that anymore. What am I trying to prove? Of course, I say that, but talk means shit. Don't take my word for it until it's late on a Saturday and I'm out of lines on a blonde, and I can hear Lord Daniels callin' me from across the bar—that's what'll indicate progress, if any.

I've always thought that the subway, for some reason, is the perfect place to read. Go figure. I mean, it's a million times louder than the Red and Tan bus I took back to the city, but it's a productive, stimulating noise, if that means anything. And here I am reading about Stevens, the implacable English butler, and there are five seats in a row across the aisle that no one is sitting in because there's a brown puddle of puke sloshing over all of them. There's this wonderful granola-type kid who's sitting one seat away from the lake. He probably figured out the physics of it all, and is like, "Fuck it—that shit ain't gonna spill over one more—and I want to sit the fuck down." I admire that type of bravery. It's funny 'cause everyone is looking at the vomit and rolling their eyes or turning up their noses in disgust. You won't catch my ass doing that, man, because I mean, a couple of nights ago, that would have been mine, right? I been there before. But this book is excellent, and there's a great-looking woman standing up straphanging—remember what I told you before, kid, I don't stand for *anybody*—and you're gonna hate me for this, but I kind of tilt the cover of my book over to her so she can see it, man, so she knows I ain't reading *Dianetics* or some John Grisham thing. Not that there's anything wrong with Grisham, 'cause I done him twice, I think; it's just that reading the bastard won't make me stand out, you know what I mean? But I don't care if I was reading a book that this girl fuckin' *wrote,* man, 'cause she ain't impressed with my ass, and she rolls her eyes until Twenty-third Street, and then she rolls on out of there.

I get out on West Fourth, like I said, and the smell of stale vomit disappears and gives way to the smell of vinegar going through the whole station. I'm out of there, and everything I love about New York is right within sight, man. There are the hard-core pickup basketball games. I told you I'm not into sports, which is true, but sometimes I check out the games so I can listen to the language the players use and the way they argue. It's funny, 'cause they run one play, then they fight about it and discuss it for twenty minutes, and then they finally get around to running another play. It's funny when they argue what the score is—it's like the great mathematics professors goin' toe to toe over a formula (math: that could be my answer to everything). Beautiful stuff. Some of those games can draw big-ass crowds; you'd be surprised. And there's the movie theater where I saw *Of Mice and Men*—not the old one, the classic, but the one with John Malkovich and Gary Sinise—somehow that changed my life. I don't know, kid, I guess it had something to do with the way Sinise said things. That was the start of me seeing movies all by myself. Actually, I got into a huge fight with Leonia that night, so *I* stormed out of the room (usually it was her) and went ahead and saw the movie. I cooled down and went back to the room, and she says, "Where've you been?" And I say that I saw *Of Mice and Men,* and then she says, "What? You were supposed to see that movie with me!" And I tell her that I hate her, and ba-boom, I'm out the door again, but this time for all night. She specialized sometimes in saying the wrong things at the wrong time.

But I droop down from West Fourth and Sixth Avenue over to Bleecker, where I can walk real slow and really soak everything in, especially the people. It's still early, but it's already dark. Damn, ever notice that when you're alone, a lot of people around you seem to be laughing their asses off all the time? I swear, I see these two guys leaning on each other for support, they're cracking up so much. I almost want to go over and ask 'em to say the joke again, but that's not the type of thing people really appreciate these days, I don't think. So people are hooting up and down Bleecker, and I'm just driving on, trying to get some kind of recollection about a couple of nights ago, but it ain't really working. I cross over to the south side of the street when I get near Terra Blues, not 'cause I don't want to see the bouncer and confront him, don't get me wrong, but just 'cause I don't even want to fuckin' think about it right now. The last thing I want to see is a vomit stain on the sidewalk with my DNA plastered all over it. Vomit stains always come in the shape of Utah. I'd just rather keep an even keel, if at all possible. I'd rather think about Michelle, and the night we had together, and the possibility of one more night like that. Just one. Man, even the idea that that night won't ever happen again—it just makes me feel emptier than you can even imagine. What, do I have to go out on a limb to tell her that I enjoyed it? Do I have to run the risk of scaring her? I *did* enjoy it, damn it, since when did that become such a controversial feeling to have? You want me to really fuck her up, I'll go ahead and tell her that I fell in love with her that night. Ain't that a laugh? Let's see what she does when I say that!

When I get to Elizabeth Street, things start to click a little bit for me, and there's that big apartment building on the corner that I presume to contain the portion of the stairwell where I made love to Michelle. You gotta understand my situation, going back like this. I know you may not see any reason to do this kind of shit, to re-enter the fire, but you don't think about someone this much if you don't love her, do you? I just want to sleep next to her like I did before—I don't even give a shit about any of the other stuff, I swear to you. And cars scream through the intersection so I gotta actually wait until the Walk sign—God, imagine what that does to my self-image—and then I cross over. Shit, man, I don't know this chick's last name; I don't know what floor she's on; and remember, I'm still only trusting my hunch that this is the right building. It really could have been any-where. I look around to make sure no one's on my ass for any kind of reason, because I know people don't like you just loitering around their buildings for no reason, especially looking for a chick that isn't expecting you, you know? This is the nineties, and I know behavior like that could end up on the cover of newspapers. And X-Man, how long does that fucker hold a grudge, I wonder. But I try the door and it's locked. I pull harder, like that's gonna do anything, but dude, I am all locked out. I guess it's just as well, seeing as how I don't know where the hell I'm going once I go in. Why did I try the door anyway? And why the second time?

So I look over to the side of the door where all the buzz-ers for the apartments are, and I gotta tell you, there's proba-bly nine thousand people, all listed alphabetically. I mean, I don't even know where to start. I don't mean to be racist, and I'm not trying to piss anyone off, but I'm looking for as many Asian names as possible, and there are quite a few. Now, this is probably stupid, because one of my buddies in college is Korean, and his last name is Anderson, so who's to say? Was Juliet right after all: what the fuck is in a name anyway? So there are a dozen Lees, a couple Kwans, a couple Chins, and even a Shin. Now, I want to hang out with the girl, but you're nuts if you think I'm just going to sit around all night plugging buttons and asking for Michelle. And waiting around is a little silly—she might still be in the stairwell passed out, for all I know. So I peer into the door, just in case she's on her way out, and I can see that there are a lot of mirrors in the lobby, which jogs my memory back to the night. But what does that mean? A lot of lobbies have a lot of mirrors, man. Anyway, Michelle is nowhere around; it looks like I'm the only person who's on the way out. Standing right there, I'm telling you I can feel the excitement and nervousness draining out of my body and turning into the simple realization that I am standing in front of a building for no real reason at all. Times like this, you're pretty sure the whole world is looking at you, wondering why you do the things you do, so I wheel around and head towards the Bleecker entrance for the 6 train uptown. I'm about five steps on my way, before I stop dead in my tracks and head back to the buzzer to see if there's an "Ishiguro" on the roster of the apartment building, 'cause he was the cat who wrote this great book I'm reading. But nah, closest is an Iverson, and Michelle Iverson doesn't have much of a flow at all, so I'm gone.

On the train uptown, I don't really break out my book at all. It's another great opportunity to read, but it's an even better opportunity to think, so I'm thinking a lot about the play Isabel was in. I already told you that I'm not that into drama, or fake drama at least, but I gotta tell you, man, I am really, really happy that I saw that play, and not just 'cause Isabel was so good and she's my sister and everything like that. Something about the way people have been telling that great story for all these years makes me happy to be part of the tradition. The only troubling thing is that if I was a real life Romeo—or a real life Juliet, I guess, to be more accurate—and I would have come home to find my soul mate dead, I would have taken that same damn gun and done myself in. That would have been the noble and romantic thing to do, right? Difference is that Juliet really killed herself *for* Romeo, not *because* of the dude, you know? If she had killed herself 'cause Romeo had mistreated her, man, there's no telling what Romeo would have done. No telling, but I'm sure he would have handled it a little better than I did, running all over town making a jerk of myself. But the one line that I don't think ever gets quoted, that I don't think high school seniors write in their yearbooks, that I don't think men tell women on picnics in the Catskills, is the one line that really stuck with me from that play. The Prince, who I think was played by the guy I might have known back in school, is talking about how everyone was to blame by being in this family feud type of situation, indirectly causing the death of these two beautiful young people, and he's being all stern and everything, and then he turns around at us, the crowd, and screams, man, *hollers,* "All are punished!" And he says "punish-ed" with the extra syllable tacked on, which I can't get enough of. When he said that, man, I saw a bunch of people sit back in their chairs, a little startled, and the skin crawled on my arms like there were cockroaches in my armpits. I don't know why that line hit me just then, other than that he yelled it loud, but when I was walking home, man, I realized that those three words really suited my whole situation. I mean, when Leonia kills herself, who really wins?

OK, there were definitely things I could have done a little differently, I'll be the first to announce that on national TV. I mean, sometimes I would drink a little, and I might have told you, I express my anger in a way that isn't always the most productive. And you know, she wasn't the biggest girl or anything, so I'm sure that freaked her out a little. Not only that, though, but when things weren't getting a little bit physical, I wasn't always that responsive to every one of her needs—I'll come right out and say that. Hey, I never said I was the world's best guy, or the best boyfriend or roommate in the world. I'm not here to argue about that. Plus, if you're like me, and you really know how to get a message across with words, how to push people's buttons, it's pretty easy to intimidate them. Man, I'm not too proud of that.

And I'm sure if you asked Leonia, she would admit that she fucked up quite a bit, too. She made every effort in her power to drive me insane and to distract me from shit that she knew was important to me. I don't know how two people who loved each other could try to make the other one fail. We were so jealous and competitive—it was really a shame. Man, and she was the first one who always wanted to be a team, like me and her could take on the world, which we probably could have, but of course, who's to say now? Only thing, now when she's on my mind, it's like all my moves are trapped in sand, weighing me down, making me feel old and slow. Ah, what do you care about all that? Stop me before I embarrass myself. All I'm trying to say is that I got punished 'cause Leonia died; Leonia got punished 'cause she died; her family did 'cause they can't talk to her or see her anymore; my family did 'cause now I'm kind of fucked up; and everyone who I'm ever going to come across for the next little while is going to feel something of the pain I felt. I mean, I can't just shrug it off every night, you know? That would be unhealthy. So it's really a kind of awful chain reaction if you stop to think about it, and it ends up punishing everyone who's even remotely involved. I think that's what the Prince in *Romeo and Juliet* meant, only notice how clean he said it?

After me on autopilot gets to my apartment, I pause for a few seconds before I break my keys out. I'll tell you, I don't know what it is, but here I am, my insides sore, my ear throbbing, and lonely as a motherfucker, but I'm telling you, I'm not dreading going inside. Truth is, I got to go to the bathroom pretty bad, and I do need to get in. So I key my way in there, and take the right turn to the bathroom. On the way in I toss my jacket on the chair, and it's not until I sit down on the toilet that I realize—shit!—I left *The Remains of the Day* in the side pocket. What a blown opportunity! I guess that means I have nothing to do except wait for the shit to come out, and to think about the bathroom and all. Damn, this room has seen enough blood, the last thing it needs is more coming out of my ass, do you know what I'm saying? My eyes are kind of blurry, but I do try to zone in on the tiles of the floor, trying to remember where the shape of her body was sprawled, trying to see some faint aspects of blood. Dude, it wasn't like a TV detective show or anything like that; there was no interrogation or chalk outline, except for maybe the chalk outline of my heart. No, cops came in and out in like an hour, no more than two—all business.

Officers came, called homicide people, and they called some more specialists to officially declare her dead, to sign the certificate. Can you believe they had to call more people in, like you needed some expert to determine that the girl was dead? A few people asked me a couple of questions, and that was that. I mean, I fixed 'em all ice water. I don't know how to make coffee—that was Leonia's job, and you know I didn't have any crullers to pass out. I think they should give policemen some kind of training on how to be a little nicer in situations like that. Or maybe they didn't know if I killed her, or whatever. One guy was kind of understanding, asking me where I could be reached for further questioning, telling me he'd call me if he needed me, but he didn't think it would be necessary. Who knows what goes through their minds, man? There's just no telling.

But here on the toilet, I don't even remember eating all that much and my body is just churning out whatever kinds of things I have in there, and I start sweating a little bit. Man, I remember when I used to do the littlest things easy, no problem, and now I can't do anything without it being a big deal. That's kind of why I'm not in a hurry to start calling people up or seeing them. I mean, remember Nicole? Little meetings can turn out to be the biggest, most cata-fuckin'-clysmic thing, so I just better not. I was probably tempting the Fates when I went in and tried to bum rush Michelle's apartment. If I went up there, I'd probably interrupt her giving a blow job to the bouncer at Terra or something like that; would have been all I needed. I ain't mentioning this just gratuitously, guy, but Michelle gave me a blow job that I can still fuckin' feel! Three days later! I mean, she went after the tip of my dick with her front two teeth like she was trying to gnaw open a stubborn bag of potato chips or something. It hurt so much that I was laughing. It *burns* to piss now. So I wasn't going to mention this, but you can add my penis to all those other things that need a break, a little bit of time to recuperate. I mean, Jesus, the pain in my head is fuckin' *unrelenting!* But it's time to wipe, and I delay a little bit, just kind of thinking about shit.

For some reason, sitting there on the toilet bowl, maybe 'cause I mentioned my penis, I'm thinking about my fourth-grade teacher that got busted for molesting my friend. I was going to be a character witness on behalf of my teacher, but my mom wouldn't let me. She said I couldn't because we had to visit my grandparents in New York City. I suppose I was too young then, but I know now it was really because my ma knew that the guy had done it, and she didn't want to tell me. Like I couldn't figure that shit out after a few months, the way kids talk on the blacktop? A lot of people felt bad for the teacher, saying he must have had some problems, but I want you to think about me, and think about the kid that got fondled. I'm talking about permanent, Gulf War-type damage. I mean, nine years old is a rough age to start writing a coming of age story. Shit, after Leonia killed herself, I guess I'm here to say that twenty-fuckin'-one is even too young to write one of those. Well, why the fuck am I thinking about my teacher now, stud? Now's not the time. And I get up and wipe, and it feels horrible and goopy, but I look at the paper, and—*brown,* kid, all brown, the way brown looks on the motherfuckin' Crayola box. I stare at that thing for a little bit, wondering when I've ever seen such a majestic, beautiful sight in my life. I wonder what exactly my body did to all the poison (was it just the Daniels? the stress? my family?). I guess I donated it all to the New Jersey sewage system; New York's is bad enough without me adding to it. So I finish up and then I flush, and I look at that as a wonderful contribution to the ocean, or wherever the fuck that shit ends up going.

But now is probably the best time to apologize, if I have to, for harshing on my folks a little bit. It dawns on me that maybe the best thing that could have happened out of my trip home is that my folks ignored me a little bit, that they weren't communicative, that they weren't all emotional. They were just my folks. Normal. Anything else, and it would have been fake. And I can't stand fake.

But I gotta say, I put some water to boil for some spinach fettuccine, 'cause I'm kind of hungry, and that takes a while. I got a few minutes to rummage around the place. One of these days, despite whatever I said before, it sure would be nice to find a suicide note or something; you know, some new information from Leonia that I never had before. I doubt it's gonna come any time soon, though, plus I don't think Leonia's the type of person to hide shit. I don't even have that many pictures of her or anything. We lived in this apartment, 4D, for eight months, until enough was enough, I guess. But as I'm getting everything squared away, just straightening things up a little, I'm like an archaeologist, uncovering layers of my existence as I clean the room. I'm not the type of guy that needs everything to be amazingly neat, but if it gets too messy, well then I get in a bad mood, and I can't function at all. I just need it so it looks like I respect myself, like I have a little dignity.

Soon enough, the water starts boiling—I can hear the anger of all the molecules from the other room—and in goes the pasta. I clear off the table, all the days of *The New York*

Times; man, that fuckin' paper seems so indispensable at eight in the morning, but the next day it takes up so much space, you just wish it would evaporate. But then I see something under the table and I bend down to pick it up—a Styrofoam cup. Why the fuck would one of those be in my place, man? I use glass. And it's got coffee stains inside, and, like, lipstick on the rim of it, red lipstick. That's kind of funny, because Leonia didn't really wear lipstick, and when she did, it was kind of brown, sort of like brick. I'd say the cup belonged to one of the cops, only thing there were no women cops, just male donut-chompers. That red, dude, shining, still, like a brand spankin' new fire engine, kind of like the kind Julie wears, Julie from work.

Julie, man. Damn. And the cloud of guilt and sadness just washes over me like poison and blood. This is how it must feel to die, my friend, this is how it must feel in your last second of life. I take the gun out, which I've grown used to pokin' out of my crotch, you know, taking it out and putting it in automatically whenever I got to. So I take it out and check it out from a million different angles. Billy the Kid, man, Bernhard Goetz. They used this thing like artists use paint brushes—Leonia same way, I think. Are you saying that Pablo Picasso ever made a grander statement with a brush than Leonia did with this little gun? Fuck that! Art, suicide, what's the difference? One is easy to frame; the other makes you cry and wonder at the same time. That's my take on it. But I got this gun in my hand, still, and you know what? It feels heavy. Maybe it's the lead inside, but it feels awkward and heavy, and I put the instrument down on the table with a definitive clack. Finally my crotch feels cool, the way it's supposed to. No reason to be lugging that shit around. Should have let the cops take that thing. If you have a gun and you're not ready to use it, you're about a million times worse off than if you're just you—I guess I learned something after all. Goddamned gun.

Well, the gun may be gone, but my thoughts, recent ones now, are weighing me down like you wouldn't believe. I feel like this apartment's a friggin' boxing ring, or something. I know I got to deal with it in here, I can't go outside to fight all my external contenders; I gotta stay here and take care of business, so to speak. But I'm sitting there and all of a sudden, my motherfuckin' peripheral vision squawks up again, rearing it's curious head. And I can see something that I can't believe I haven't seen in all the time I was here already—the red light of my answering machine blinking with one solitary message. Blink. Pause. Blink. Pause. Blink. If it's the eye of the Cyclops, you can't tell if it's winking or blinking at you. Damn, it sure seems like it's makin' some sort of fun of me. Imagine if *I* was electronic? If I made myself electronic, I could let myself go like that, be rhythmic, go through life on one monotonous beat, signaling to people one thing in one fashion. Damn, I think I could do that, I'm telling you. Piece of cake. But you know what I'd rather do? I'd rather pull you to the side if I have to, like now, to tell you sometimes (not always, man, don't worry) that I'm hurting a little bit, and that I need an ear or two, something like that. Because, man, this blood running around my veins, in, out, through, outside of, sometimes, is totally tainted. I know it is. No half-assed odyssey is going to change that, at least not for now. OK? So I got no problem with putting the gun away, putting the whiskey away, you know, putting the harshness, and maybe even some of the curses away. I'll get a new harmonica and play you a song, if you want me to. Whatever you want. I just wanna say, sometimes, with Leonia, I can look right in your eyes and tell you I don't remember anything about her. Sometimes, I can't see her face at all, I don't remember anything we did together, I don't remember any of her habits. Leonia is just a name to me. Other times, I'll just think of the strangest thing, the last thing you'd expect me to remember, like the way her voice would get on the phone when I called her out of the blue, and I just knew how happy I'd made her. How come I remember that kind of random stuff? I ain't gonna argue—the only thing I don't want my mind to settle in on is all the bad shit that went on, all the times that were so wasteful, 'cause that's a dead-end street if ever there was one.

And you know things are a little more normal when you stop welcoming the distractions, and they become irritations. Shit, I hope you know, if you want distractions, just rent a New York City apartment, let me tell you—you'll get more than your fill. 'Cause down the hall there's this newborn baby who I've been hearin' express himself for the last two or three months. I'm not sure I've ever even seen him, but we've had conversations all night long: him yelling for food or something, and me moaning for quiet. Now his wailing is just bouncing up and down the empty hallway. Distractions? That fuckin' blinking red light is distracting the shit out of me, man, driving me crazy. Wait, let me first just go get my fettuccine, 'cause it looks ready, and like I said before, kid, I'm hungry; what do you want me to do?

Anyway, that's that; I didn't even mean to keep you this long, but you know how things are—you know the way it goes. I can't say I told you every single thing, every last detail, but that's okay. It's always healthiest to save some things for next time. Oh wait—I can't believe it—I never told you, my name is Sam. Jeez, it totally slipped my mind. For real, man, I'm really sorry about that. Why do I keep doing things like that? I can't believe how I always forget the most important things!

Mark Cirino was born in New York City in 1971.
This is his first novel.